Those Others

NAVIGATING THE "RIDDLE OF HOMOSEXUALITY" IN 1965

A NOVEL

J O E   O P E N S H A W

This book is a work of fiction, based on historical figures and events.

ISBN: 1450532012
ISBN-13: 9781450532013
Library of Congress Control Number: 2010900804

For information on purchasing this book, or for author interviews, visit www.thoseothersthebook.com or find the author on Facebook or twitter (@joebessemer)

BOP Publishing
Bessemer, AL

In Memory of

Richard Devan
Washington, DC

For Uncle Joe—
Without your forethought and inspiration,
this work would not have been conceived

With thanks to
Frank Kameny

And special thanks to Bobby,
for his understanding and support
during this effort

Preface

Between January 31 and February 4, 1965, a series of articles regarding homosexuality was published in the *Washington Post.* These five articles were the inspiration for this novel, and they have been reprinted in their entirety at the end of the book. The articles deal with homosexuality from many aspects, including the social, medical, psychiatric, employment, legal, and religious aspects. Most likely this was the first publication in the mainstream media that presented homosexuality in what at the time could be considered a fair and balanced way.

Regardless, the series was bound to have affected many who read it. Some would be shocked to open their Sunday paper and see the headline:

Those Others: A Report on Homosexuality

They may have been more shocked to read about the controversial behavior of some homosexuals or the severe punishments that were handed down to those unfortunate enough to get caught practicing their behavior.

It may have been their first introduction to what the Kinsey report said about the subject. That, in turn, could have led to questions about themselves...or their spouses.

On the other hand, the articles could have given encouragement to homosexuals living in the DC area. They might have read for the first time that homosexuals could lead a normal life and that at least one state had exempted homosexual acts from legal penalty. And they might have learned that a local group, the Mattachine Society, was working for their rights in their city.

Some, however, may have been left confused by the articles, especially in the reports on the possible causes and treatments of homosexuality.

Now, almost forty-five years later, private consensual homosexual acts are no longer criminal in this country, and while advances in medicine, psychiatry, and science have increased our knowledge of the origins and so called "ex-gay" therapies have been discredited, we find ourselves still having to debate the same issues of employment discrimination, violence, religious acceptance, and partnership recognition that existed in the 1960s.

The year 1965 was historic in that civil rights and social unrest in general led to massive demonstrations. The march from Selma to Montgomery occurred that year, as did the first large-scale anti–Vietnam War protest in Washington, DC. In addition, the first gay rights protest in Washington, DC, occurred in front of the White House, where about ten picketers marched with signs demanding equality in the workplace.

But let's go back a few months, back to January of that year, when a young man, confused about his life, began his discovery.

Prologue

January 2, 1965

In a small town in Tennessee, a teenage boy boards a bus headed for Washington, DC, to find direction for his life.

At Brown Chapel in Selma, Alabama, Martin Luther King Jr. delivers an address to give direction to a movement.

In Washington, DC, members of the Eighty-ninth Congress are gathering to begin their historic session.

One

A sliver of sunlight crept across the dimly lit room, and as it reached Michael's face, he opened his eyes. Drapes that should have blocked the light from entering had not been pulled together well the night before. At home in Tennessee, the window in the bedroom he shared with his brother also faced east, and often small beams of early morning light would pierce the darkness for the same reason.

He was accustomed to waking up early—farm life dictated that. He thought he heard someone moving about, but half asleep, he rolled over away from the light and began to think about where he might be.

He was alone in bed and couldn't see anything in the room to remind him where he was. The air felt chilly. He pulled the cover up close to his chin and stared at the ceiling. He closed his eyes and wished his headache would go away.

As he held a pillow, he imagined arms wrapped around him, the warmth of someone pressed close to him. *Just a few more minutes*, he thought. The warmth he was feeling was from a thick blanket, however, and not the person he imagined. This was so different from what he was accustomed. He thought of the quilts he had to use to keep warm in bed in the cold, drafty house in Tennessee. Three, sometimes four thick quilts would pin him to the sheet on a cold night, but he would be warm. The quilts had been made by his grandmother, and the knowledge of that made the warmth more than just physical.

Now he was in this big bed, even bigger than his parents' bed. The room was now light enough that he noticed a large mirror hanging over the dresser across the room past the foot of the bed. He raised his head up enough to see over the footboard, and he could see himself. There was no mirror in his room at home, so seeing himself in bed was new. He looked oddly alone, framed in the reflection, almost, by the large bedposts. He imagined himself to be important, in some way, in that big bed. He shifted back and sat up against the headboard, allowing the covers to fall down to his waist. He stared at the reflection and brought a hand up to feel the hair that was beginning to grow on his chest. Rubbing his hand across it, and then his stomach, he watched himself in the mirror. He was suddenly reminded of an incident that had occurred a year earlier. He had been lying naked on his bed when his mother opened the door and walked in as he was rubbing his chest in the same manner while exploring his body. The memory of his mother seeing him naked and giving himself pleasure caused him to grab the bedspread with both hands and pull it up over himself, and the shame he had felt at the time returned. He slid back down under the covers and rolled over onto his stomach.

His thoughts of his mother shifted to a memory of her holding back tears as he boarded the bus in Nashville to come here. Nashville had seemed so big—after all, it was the state capital—but it was nothing like this, the nation's capital.

His mother had driven him to Nashville from their farm near Franklin, but it was his father who had the connections to get him here. His dad had served in the Army Air Corps with Tennessee's junior senator, Ross Bass, fighting together in "the Big One," as he used to call it. The plan had been for Michael to follow his father's path into the military, but worsening asthma during his senior year changed all that. He was good at basketball and played on his high school's team, but again, the asthma kept the colleges from considering a scholarship, so there would be no future in college, either.

Michael had worked on the family farm since he was a child, and after high school graduation, he had assumed that would be his life. He enjoyed it. His family owned a little over one hundred and fifty acres of rolling pastureland and hay fields, and as far back as he could remember, tending the cattle and putting up hay was what he did. His father seemed resigned to letting Michael stay on the farm if military service was not an option. In his father's eyes, an ailment that kept one from serving in the military, or even from developing as an athlete, was a sign of weakness. But Michael was anything but weak. Years of tossing bales of hay around and pounding fence posts into the ground had resulted in Michael developing into a fit young man. No one would assume him to be weak.

He had turned eighteen during the summer after graduating from high school. By the fall of the year, he had decided that working on the farm after school and in the summer was OK, but the thought of doing it for the rest of his life left him depressed. It was lonely work, and he missed the camaraderie of his school friends. He wanted to be around people.

So his father called his old army buddy and arranged for Michael to meet him in Washington for what was supposed to be a two-week stay to expose the young man to opportunities that could help "build your character" and "give you direction," as Michael remembered.

He arrived in Washington on January 2, 1965, the day before the Eighty-ninth Congress was to begin its historic session. Four weeks later he was still there, and on Sunday, January 31, he woke up in the bed of a United States senator.

"Shit. Shit, shit, shit," he said in a whisper, getting louder with each repetition of the word after remembering where he was. He had not meant to spend the night here. He didn't even know whose house he was in. The man had introduced himself, but Michael couldn't remember his name. Or had he even given a name? No, he only said he was a senator.

"What in the world have I done?" he muttered. "Created a fuckin' mess, that's what," he answered himself with his next breath.

He felt like he was trapped. Not in this house, but in a situation from which he knew no escape. He thought back to how this had come about.

Two weeks after arriving, while walking along the mall near the Washington Monument at night, he had been followed for several minutes. Michael stopped and sat on a bench, and a moment later a stranger approached and stood directly in front him, his hands on his hips. Michael looked up and saw a man, not much older than himself, in tight blue jeans, a white T-shirt, and a leather jacket. His eyes continued to move up until he was looking the man in his eyes. A half hour later, Michael walked back to his motel, having had his first sexual experience.

Michael rolled out of bed, pulled his pants on, and walked to the window, squinting at the sun that had brightened up the room. He spread his left hand across his eyes and put his thumb and middle finger on his temples and applied pressure. He listened but could not tell if anyone was close by or not. He really needed to pee, he realized, remembering the scotch whiskey he had drunk for the first time a few hours before, so he found his way to a bathroom. While standing at the toilet, he heard a noise and turned his head and saw the senator standing in the doorway in pajamas and a bathrobe. He suddenly remembered why he was here.

Michael had not gone out looking for sex the night before, or even the first time. Two weeks ago it had happened by accident. Afterwards he felt ashamed. No one could ever know what he had done, and he swore he would never do that again. But the following Saturday he returned to the same bench, hoping to find the same man. He didn't find him, and he returned to his motel in a state of confusion. How could he have gone out purposely looking for something that he felt was not right? But he still had a strong desire for another orgasm like he'd had the week before.

He masturbated. It was not for the first time, but it was the first time he had given himself such pleasure with the knowledge of what it was like with another man. He imagined he was with the stranger and that it was that man's hand that grasped him and brought him to climax. His satisfaction was short-lived, however, and his sense of confusion returned.

So on this night he had mixed feelings about the two previous Saturdays, and after supper he had decided to return to his room. He chose a route that avoided the mall, and he walked past the Capitol building instead. But when he reached the Capitol, he walked around the building so he could see the Washington Monument, and while staring down the mall, a man in a suit approached him.

"Young man," he had said, "you look lost."

"No, just on my way home," Michael replied. "Well, not home really, to a motel room."

"Visiting, huh," the man said. "Where, then, is home?"

"Tennessee, just south of Nashville. We have a farm."

"Ah, Senators Gore and Bass—both good men, even if they are from the wrong party," he laughed. "I serve in the Senate with them. What brings you to the capital?"

At the mention of Senator Bass, Michael turned and looked at the man, an older man who looked official to him in his dark suit, standing in front of the Capitol. "Oh, I just wanted to look at the Washington Monument on my way..."

"No, not the Capitol. The capital *city*, DC. What brings you here?"

"Oh, my dad arranged for me to come so I could, uh, develop a plan for my life, I guess. He got Senator Bass to help me; they flew together in the war."

The senator motioned for Michael to walk, and they started in the direction of his motel. The conversation kept Michael interested, and he turned with the senator and followed him to his car; without questioning, Michael got in.

He remembered riding to a nice neighborhood, nicer than the area where his motel was. The senator apologized for neglecting to take Michael straight home, and he invited him in to continue their conversation and have a drink.

"OK, but only if you'll drive me back in an hour," Michael agreed. They went inside.

The night had passed, and now Michael felt embarrassed standing half-naked and urinating in front of the senator; he could feel himself turning red. He tried to cover himself as he finished his business.

"You weren't that shy last night," the senator laughed. "Listen, when you're finished, come downstairs—there's something I want you to see."

Michael really felt a sense of disappointment in himself and wanted to leave. He wanted to be alone. He couldn't even remember what had happened in bed, in part because he had been drunk, but also because he didn't want to remember. But he knew he couldn't get out of the man's house easily. He made his way down the stairs and into the kitchen, where the senator was sitting and drinking coffee. He offered Michael a cup, but Michael refused, saying, "I really need to leave," as he started back toward the door.

"Wait. Don't leave just yet. Besides, you wouldn't know how to get back, would you? Look, I want you to see this."

The senator handed Michael the Sunday paper with section E on top, folded so that the bottom half of the page was what Michael saw.

Those Others: A Report on Homosexuality

The bold headline in the *Washington Post* was staring Michael in the face.

"Sit down. You might want to read this."

"I am *not* homosexual," Michael said, looking down.

"Listen, Michael." Michael was surprised that the man called him by name. "Last night you had a few drinks, and you may not have realized what you were doing, but you sure acted like a homosexual. You told me a little bit about your experience in the park two weeks ago and seemed concerned, but even with that, I could see that you were getting aroused. By the time we went upstairs, I could tell you wanted more than the anonymous kind of sex you had in the park. I don't know that I can give you that, Michael, other than allowing you to put a face with what you're doing."

The senator continued, speaking with authority. "You had a need last night, just as I did. We took care of it."

Michael buried his head in his hands and rested his elbows on the table. "I should never have come here. I should have stayed on the farm. This is not who I want to be. It's not who I am." He looked up, his eyes red. "What about you? Then you're a homosexual?"

"No," the senator quickly replied. "I'm married, and I have two children."

"Well what do you mean, we 'took care of it,' if you aren't a homo?" Michael felt sick. This was not helping his headache, and now his stomach was reacting. He realized he had had sex with this man, a man his father's age. He didn't remember the details, but he imagined waking up next to this man and looked away.

The senator replied as if he had rehearsed for this moment. "I am not a homosexual, but I do on occasion feel the need to be with a man. There is an urge that my wife simply can't satisfy. But I do not cheat on her; I have never been with another woman."

"I don't understand. I don't understand myself, and I sure don't understand what you just said!" Michael stood up and immediately sat back down, rubbing his thumb and finger against his eyes and pressing tears onto his cheeks. "I just don't understand this."

The senator took a deep breath. "Michael, listen." He had a commanding voice. "To be frank with you, I don't understand it either. But from my viewpoint—listen, I don't want you repeating this to anyone, you hear—but for me, I have to have a wife. So I fell in love."

He sat in the chair next to Michael. "I got married. If I were going to be elected as a mayor, later as a representative, and now as a senator, I had to be seen as a family man. You're young. Things are changing. That's why I thought you might want to see this article in the *Post*. The writer asks several questions."

He picked up the paper and began reading aloud. "Are homosexuals born or made by environment? Is homosexuality a crime, disease, choice or natural way of life for a minority? Are there more homosexuals today than heretofore, and do they pose a threat to the structure and moral fiber of society? Can homosexuality be treated, and if it can, should it be?"

The senator stopped reading and looked up at Michael. "There are more questions, Michael—questions here that have never been asked in public before. And answers as well. For someone like you, someone young, with no wife or girlfriend, someone who can build a life around who they are rather than who they are required to be, this report should be of great interest."

Michael sat silently for a few moments, wiped his face, and then turned to the senator. "Sir, with all due respect, if I'm hearing you right, you brought me here, liquored me up, had your way with me, and now you feel qualified to give me advice about how I should live my life? Yes, I came to Washington to get direction for my life like I told you last night, but I have been pulled in a direction that I knew nothing about, and it's not where I want to go. I can't.

"You know, I was only supposed to stay here for two weeks. But that Sunday morning after I...after *that* happened...well, after that I couldn't get on that bus and go home and see my mother. I couldn't face her. She would know. So I called her and lied to her. I told her Senator Bass had found me a job that would allow me to stay here a while longer. But I didn't have a job. Yeah, I do now, thanks to Mr. Bass, but until I called her, I had not even thought about a job or about staying. I am not a liar, sir—I have never lied to my mother before, but having sex like that and the shame that followed caused me to lie to her. And everyone I see—Senator Bass, the others in his office—I feel like they know what I've done. I feel cheap, and this isn't helping."

Michael thought for a moment and then said, "If I went home, I feel like my mom and dad and my brother would know as well. And I would have to lie to deny it, all because of what happened in that park. And add to that what happened last night. I don't know why I do it.

"And you. I know I drank too much last night. But still, what we did, I really don't even remember. You say I had sex with you. Don't take offense, but the thought of it is making me sick. I mean, I don't know why I like it. Doing that. I shouldn't. But doing it with you makes me *know* that I shouldn't.

"So I don't know what to do. But I do know this—I want to go back to my motel. Will you take me back to where you picked me up?"

Michael didn't want the senator to know where he was staying.

He looked back up as the senator began to speak.

"Michael, I had no idea you weren't more self-aware. I mean, I know you told me that the anonymous sex you had near the mall was your first time, but I thought you were more accepting of your feelings and just not accustomed to acting on them.

"And I didn't pour the liquor down your throat, if you remember. I offered you one glass, and you refilled it yourself—what three, four times? I don't know, but don't put all the blame about the way you feel on me."

Michael remembered who he was with and decided he had better show the man some respect, seeing that his boss was a colleague of the senator.

"I'm sorry, sir; I didn't mean to blame you. I'm just really disappointed in myself—it's not about you. Can you just take me back to the Capitol?"

The senator agreed to take him, and as they were about to walk out of the house, Michael turned and walked back to the kitchen and picked up the newspaper.

"Can I take this?" he asked.

Two

Michael found that he could immerse himself in work at Senator Bass's office, and he had learned more about government there in a few weeks than he had all through school. He found both government and its history fascinating, but most of his work involved menial tasks such as answering the phone and greeting visitors. In his spare time he read books from the senator's office—books, he learned, that were gifts from other officials and constituents and, for the most part, had never been opened.

He was amazed at the money he made working what to him seemed part-time. He was used to farm work, sunup to sundown, and no pay. "Early to bed and early to rise," his mom used to say, "makes a man healthy, wealthy, and wise." That always amused him because he sure wasn't getting wealthy hauling hay and chasing cattle from one pasture to the next. And his dad didn't seem to be doing too well, either, so he took his mother's advice cautiously.

He was surprised at the number of Negroes in the building where he worked. He had rarely seen black people—only when the family made trips to Nashville might they come across them. And certainly he had never spoken to one. Some of the senators had Negroes on their staffs, and many frequently had visitors who were black. Michael knew little about the struggle that was going on for civil rights, but he quickly learned that major legislation was being prepared to guarantee Negroes the right to vote. Since Michael was not yet old enough to vote, he had hardly considered that some were being denied that privilege. But he had at least heard of Martin Luther King Jr., who once had appeared in the building to talk with senators about the legislation. So work for Michael was full of new and educational experiences, and he was able to focus on his tasks without interruption during the day.

After his experience with the senator, however, when he was alone in his motel room at night, his thoughts focused on the problem that had developed. He tried to read, but it was too quiet and his mind would wander. A cold front that moved through made it unbearable to walk outside, so both Monday and Tuesday night he was alone in the small room with just his thoughts. Wednesday afternoon he decided he would go nuts if he had to sit in the room by himself with nothing to do, so on his way to the motel he stopped near a liquor store and paid a man five dollars to go in and get him a bottle of scotch. It had seemed to do something the other night to blur his thoughts, and besides, he sort of liked the taste.

After dinner, he returned to his room, poured himself a glass, and pulled the Sunday newspaper from beneath the mattress where he had hidden it in fear that someone would see it. He began reading.

Those Others: A Report on Homosexuality

This series of articles would not have been written five years ago. Then, a frank and open discussion of homosexuality would have been impossible. It was a topic not to be mentioned in polite society or public print because it could be distasteful, embarrassing and disturbing.

"This is supposed to make me feel better about myself?" he questioned himself out loud.

In the first few paragraphs, homosexuality was compared to mental illness and venereal disease, and it was referred to as "the problem of homosexuality," yet the article offered Michael some hope by admitting that myths and misconceptions cloud any discussion of the "problem," and that it might be time to reappraise our laws and attitudes.

He read that some homosexuals lead double lives and marry and have children, and he thought of the senator from out west who had given him the paper he was holding. He continued reading: "One isolated homosexual experience doesn't make a 'homosexual' just as one drink doesn't make an alcoholic."

He looked at the glass of scotch in his hand and thought to himself, *What about two isolated experiences? Or two drinks?*

He poured another glass.

Michael read the entire article, and when he was finished, two passages stood out to him. The article told of a government astronomer with a degree from Harvard who had lost his job because of a report that he was a homosexual. He said, "I decided then that I had run long enough. All of us have to make our own compromises in life. I decided not to hide anymore."

Reading that, and the effects of the scotch, made Michael want to accept what he might be, to not hide. *If this man, educated at Harvard, can be open about his homosexuality, then why can't I?* he thought.

The other passage was in a paragraph describing homosexuals and the police: "Or they see the man who compulsively seeks a quick partner in the park."

Michael again thought of Marlon—that's the name the man in the park had given him. He really wanted to go look for Marlon, but he was drunk—or close to it—and he didn't want to be out walking in the cold. Besides, what he read about the police frightened him.

He poured himself another glass and lay down on the bed. He thought about the words and phrases he read in the article.

Faggot. He had heard this word on the basketball court and in the locker room in reference to members of other teams. He had even used it.

Sodom and Gomorrah. He knew little about the biblical story other than it told something about somebody's wife turning into a pillar of salt.

Queens, high-drag. He had no idea what these terms meant.

Second largest minority after the Negro. He knew little about the minority status of the Negro and even less about the status of homosexuals.

Gay. "Don we now our gay apparel," the words to a Christmas song, was all he could think of. He had not heard this word in reference to homosexuals.

He lay there wondering what he was. He replayed in his mind over and over the phrase that read, "One isolated homosexual experience doesn't make a homosexual." He had had two homosexual experiences and had thought about it numerous times since that first time, even fantasized about it. At what point could he no longer deny it? He had to quit having those feelings. He felt himself becoming aroused, and this left him confused. Why would he get aroused when he was trying not to think about it? But the more he tried not to think about it, the more he thought of Marlon.

His memory recalled that night. He remembered sitting on the bench on the mall, looking into the stranger's eyes, and realizing that the stranger was massaging his crotch. His heart rate increased, but his eyes did not move. He didn't understand what was happening, and he couldn't allow himself to look, but he knew what the man was doing. He didn't move. He began to feel tingly and began to shiver. The stranger stepped closer until the hand covering his crotch was right in front of Michael's face. Michael saw the hand turn toward him, and he felt it grasp his chin and pull him into a standing position. The man leaned into him, and still holding Michael's face, he pulled it to his own. It happened so fast. Michael felt lips against his own, whiskers rubbing his cheeks, a tongue probing his mouth, a hand sliding down his chest, across his stomach, around his back, pulling them together. The stranger pressed his hardness against his own. Suddenly the man pulled back.

"Come on," he said in a deep whisper, "over here."

He led Michael between a row of hedges and some trees, and after another short kiss, he slowly dropped to his knees.

Michael could not remember what the man looked like. He remembered his eyes—deep brown, captivating. He remembered the large, strong hand that had grasped his chin and the feel of their faces together, but he couldn't remember what the man's face looked like. It had been dark, and his mind couldn't focus. It had happened so quickly, and then the man was gone. It could have been any man.

The alcohol had its effect, and Michael fell asleep. The next morning as he was getting ready for work, he tried to remember how the article had ended. On his way out, he picked up the paper and read at the end of the article, *"MONDAY: Freud's letter to a mother."* He hid the paper back under the mattress.

That night, in a bar close by, it was dark and the clientele almost all men. Most nights the bar was filled with both men and women who came to hear live music performed by locals, some of whom seemed on the brink of hitting it big. But recently, Thursday nights began attracting homosexual men, and the performances turned to men in drag, performing as women. The bar had never advertised this, but a few months prior, a performance by a man impersonating Judy Garland and singing songs from *The Wizard of Oz* got so much attention that the owner asked the performer to return the next week. Judy, whose real name was Roland, had asked his friends to spread the word, and the following week the bar was full of homosexual men there to support their friend. The regular patrons of the bar seemed willing to turn the facility over to those others one night a week, and the owner of the bar certainly liked the crowd and the money they spent.

Marlon was sitting at a table with two other men, discussing the previous weekend. These men were typical homosexuals, according to society's view. They had jobs that any man might have—Marlon was a supermarket manager, and the other men worked in healthcare. One was a doctor Marlon had known for years, and the other was a technician who had come along with his doctor friend for the first time. They had respectable jobs during the work day, but on weekends and Thursday evenings, they were what the newspaper articles had described as "predatory," a term used to describe certain men who cruise for sex. They hung out in parks, at a local bowling alley, or at this bar, in search of sex with like-minded or unsuspecting men—it didn't matter.

Marlon was not his real name, but he called himself that, after Marlon Brando, when living the homosexual side of his life. He was part of a group referred to in the *Washington Post* as the Hollywood House set who adopted pseudonyms to protect their identity and possibly their jobs.

"So, Marlon, did you meet up with that farm kid from Tennessee again?" the doctor asked.

"I went back to the same area where we met a few Saturdays before and waited for a couple of hours, but he didn't show. Damn, he was nice, too." Marlon lit a cigarette.

"Yeah, I heard about it from Doc," the third man said. "But really, you expect us to believe that you found this kid, his first time in the city, and his first time for sex? I don't know." He took Marlon's cigarette and used it to light his own.

Their conversation continued, with Marlon giving a replay of the encounter, in a lighthearted way.

"I might try to find him again this weekend," he said, picturing the young man in his mind. "Damn, he was hot. If I'm lucky, I'll tell you all about it next week."

The three looked up as the door opened and a stocky, middle-aged man walked in. "Hey, look what just walked in. Have you seen him in here before?" the doctor asked curiously.

"No. So what?" Marlon wasn't interested, still focusing on Michael.

"Well, he *is* my kind of guy," the doctor said.

"He's all yours," Marlon replied. "You know my type—young, fresh-off-the-farm yearling bulls."

They laughed since Marlon was not much older than his latest conquest, and the doctor got up and started toward the newcomer.

"You've probably scared your farm boy off," the technician said as he moved to the empty seat between him and Marlon. He put a hand on Marlon's leg. "Why don't we leave? It's getting late, and I don't think any more, uh, new prospects for you will be coming in tonight."

"Me and you?" Marlon asked. He took a long, deliberate drag on his cigarette before putting it out. "I don't see why not. Let's go out back."

The following morning at work, Michael saw a newspaper with a picture of the senator from out west on the front page. He mentioned to one of the staffers that they had met, and he inquired as to where his office was. Michael wanted to see if perhaps the senator had saved the newspaper with the article about Freud and the letter to a mother in it. He really didn't want to see the man again, but Michael thought that seeing him during the day, in his office, would be safe.

He was nervous as he entered the senator's office, and he noticed a pair of cattle horns above a painting of a mountain vista on the wall. A secretary asked his name and invited him to have a seat.

"The senator just returned from lunch, but he should be able to see you in just a few minutes if you can wait a moment. He has about fifteen minutes until his next appointment."

The secretary disappeared through a door and returned a moment later. "The senator will see you now, Michael."

She motioned him to the door, and their eyes met as he approached. She smiled and gave a half wink as he passed, and she pulled the door closed behind him.

As Michael entered the senator's office, the first thing he noticed was a picture of the man and his family. He had a daughter close to the age of Michael's brother and a son even younger. He felt a little uncomfortable as he realized this man was close to his father's age and remembered what had happened. He thought about the secretary—her look, her wink. Did she know something? Could she tell about him? That was his fear—that people would know. He began to feel uneasy and wanted to leave.

"Michael, good to see you, young man," was the senator's greeting as he stood and extended his hand. He gestured for Michael to have a seat.

Michael shook his hand. "I'd better not; I just have a question."

"Go ahead, but do have a seat. I want to know how you're doing. And how is Senator Bass?" he asked, trying to avoid seeming too personal.

"I'm doing fine. And Senator Bass is too. But listen, I want to know if you have the *Washington Post* from Monday. There was supposed to be a follow-up article to the one you gave me, and..."

"I have it, Michael, along with the other three in the series. There were five parts; the last one was yesterday."

"The one you gave me said Monday's would be about Freud and his letter to a mother. I assume that means a mother of a homosexual." He turned to make sure the door was closed. "I want to read that one."

"You should read them all, Michael. And as you feel the need, I'm sure you will. I actually have them in my briefcase; I've been carrying them around with me, thinking I might run into you here.

"I'd like to spend more time with you, Michael. I like you; I think an ongoing relationship could benefit both of us. But I want you to feel good about yourself.

"I'm going to tell you something, Michael, but it can't go any further than this room. You aren't the first young man I've known in this town. But you're the first who might have a chance at accepting what he is, and these articles can help with that."

The senator remembered a situation in which he had been involved.

"And that would benefit me; I wouldn't have to worry about my little stud turning into a nut case."

Michael sat up, surprised at the senator's abruptness. "I can't take them today. I have to go back to work." His heart began to pound, and he thought the senator could see it.

"Michael, what time do you finish up?"

"Around four thirty. It being Friday, maybe three o'clock or three thirty."

"Come back by, Michael, and I'll give you a ride back to your motel and give them to you then. Or even better, I'll take you to an early dinner and we can talk."

Michael didn't mind being called a stud, but he didn't trust the senator and didn't want him to know where to find him. And he thought about the consequences of getting into the senator's car and going to dinner with him.

"I, uh, am supposed to meet somebody after work. But I can come by here and get them if you can, uh, find something to put them in."

"Sure, Michael, I'll have them ready for you. But as you become more comfortable, I would like to see you again."

"Thank you, sir. We'll see," Michael replied, though he had no intention of seeing the man again. He rose and started out of the room.

"And Michael," the senator said, waiting for Michael to turn. "You won't tell anyone where you got them, right?"

"Yes, sir. I mean, no, sir, I won't."

"And you won't mention what I said about you and the other young men?"

"No, sir."

Three

Alone in his room that evening, Michael pulled the newspapers from the folder the senator had given him. They were in order, so Monday's paper was on top, but instead of opening it, he decided to call his mother. Michael could not imagine what he was going to read, and he wanted to speak with his own mother before he read about someone else's. He returned the papers to the folder and back under his mattress. He felt uneasy and fixed himself a glass of scotch to take the edge off before he called his mother. There was no telephone in his room, so he downed the drink and went to the motel lobby to place a collect call to his home.

Forgetting that there was a time difference, he didn't realize he would be interrupting their supper, but his mother didn't mind. He usually called on Saturday evenings to save money, so with the call coming a day early and noticing a slight change in Michael's voice, she knew something was not right. She asked him what was wrong, but Michael made up a story about having plans for Saturday night and didn't reveal anything to his mother. She ended the conversation with, "I love you, Michael, and be careful. Here's your father." Michael's father ended his short conversation with a simple, "Good-bye, son."

Michael thought he detected some uneasiness in his mother's voice during their conversation and concluded that she knew his secret. He wondered if she had told his father. After returning to his room, he locked the door and poured himself another drink.

He retrieved the folder and took out the paper with the article. The title read as follows:

Those Others – II

Scientists Disagree On Basic Nature Of Homosexuality, Chance Of Cure

"Cure?" he asked himself in a whisper. "Am I…sick?"

He read of the letter Sigmund Freud wrote in 1935: "I gather from your letter that your son is a homosexual."

Michael imagined his own mother writing such a letter.

"I am most impressed by the fact that you do not mention this term yourself in your information about him. May I question you, why do you avoid it?"

Freud said to the mother that homosexuality was not a vice, crime, or degradation, rather a "variation of the sexual function produced by a certain arrest of sexual development."

He stopped there to think. What did that mean, an "arrest of sexual development"? Sex to him was purely physical, and he wasn't aware of its emotional or psychological implications. As far as he could tell, he was fully developed sexually. And Marlon seemed to be as well.

Freud did not, he read, advocate a change to heterosexuality, which was a new term for Michael. Michael thought it a little odd that he had heard the terms "homo" and "homosexual" since junior high school, but he had never heard anyone called a "heterosexual."

Michael continued reading Freud's response. "If he is unhappy, neurotic, torn by conflicts, inhibited in his social life, analysis may bring him harmony, peace of mind, full efficiency, whether he remains a homosexual or gets changed."

The article went on to describe different approaches to homosexuality from a scientific standpoint. The article described as a "cardinal finding" that "homosexuals are not born that way but become so because of problems in the parent-child relationship—typically a domineering mother and a cold, detached father."

Michael stopped again. He didn't have many other families to compare to where he knew that much about the relationships. He thought his family was average, normal.

He did remember one teammate of his, Jack DeMent, whose father came to every game and picked them both up often after practice. Jack was surely heterosexual; he had dated the prettiest girl in school. Michael's own father had never attended a game.

And his mother—she wasn't domineering, was she? Thinking back, it was actually she who convinced his father to contact Senator Bass to make arrangements for this trip while his father seemed to think that if his son couldn't fight in the army, he should just stay at home on the farm. But did that mean anything?

He read on about different theories of development and "predisposing factors" and "pathologic conditions." A differing view was presented as well, a theory that "a man can be a homosexual and not be emotionally disturbed...normal."

He was amused by a story about an analyst who, when told by a colleague that all of the colleague's homosexual patients were ill, replied, "So are all my heterosexual patients." Were homosexuals and heterosexuals really any different?

Michael was also impressed that the analysts, as well as the author of the piece, were throwing these terms around—homosexual and heterosexual—as if in normal conversation. He looked back to see who wrote the article. Not that it would make a difference to him, but he wondered. The article had been written by Jean M. White.

This article was also Michael's introduction to the Kinsey report and its seven-point scale ranging from exclusively heterosexual to exclusively homosexual, with those in between the extremes exhibiting or practicing both traits to varying degrees.

This installment in the series gave Michael much to think about, and he would ponder it and reread it several times that evening. The article revealed that next in the series was "The Homosexual in Society," but Michael was not ready to admit to himself that he was a homosexual; after all, according to what he had read, he might just be at an "arrested" stage of development.

But there was one thing Michael was sure about. After reading and thinking about homosexuality so much, he wanted to find Marlon—but not tonight. *I might try to find him tomorrow evening since it was on a Saturday night that we...* He didn't finish his thought.

Michael was still very conflicted about his sexuality, but he began to realize that he felt better when he thought about Marlon and felt worse when he read about homosexuality being a problem.

He didn't sleep well that night, and on Saturday morning, he stayed in bed till almost noon. He spent the afternoon on the mall, with his transistor radio in his pocket and an earphone in his ear. His thoughts during the day often shifted to Marlon. Saturdays were usually reserved for sightseeing, and on this day he had planned to visit the Washington Monument. He had spent a lot of time looking at this monument and had learned quite a bit about it. Michael knew there was an elevator that could take him to the top, and he had heard that the original elevator ride took twenty minutes with wine and cheese being served along the way, something he learned from a tourist brochure.

He had to work up his nerve for this, though he really wasn't afraid of heights. After all, he had been in a Nashville skyscraper when his team had been there playing for the state championship and the teams took tours of the city. Maybe it was the perceived narrowness of the building and the way it seemed to sway when clouds moved behind it, or maybe it was the subconscious phallic symbolism of the monument that was buried somewhere in his head. Regardless, when he got to the building, his fear left him as it seemed more solid and bigger at the base than it had from a distance. And the symbolism that both drew him in and left him frightened was no longer apparent.

He rode the elevator up and was accompanied by a group of sixth graders from Missouri who were visiting as part of their school safety patrol. They thought Michael was cool with his pocket radio, and he let some of them listen with the earphone. They also seemed impressed with Michael's height—he was six foot three—and compared him to the monument itself. He enjoyed interacting with the younger kids, and when they talked their chaperone into letting them take the stairs down, he volunteered to go with them so the ladies escorting them would not have to.

The kids began counting backwards as they started down: "897, 896, 895." During the time they were on the stairs, which took a while, it began to snow outside, and by the time they reached the bottom and exited, the ground had turned white and the snow was falling heavily. The kids were out of breath when they reached the bottom, but Michael told them, "Imagine climbing up the stairs instead of coming down, how tired you would be," eliciting groaning noises from several. Michael left the kids.

"Good-bye, Mr. Washington. Good-bye, Mr. Monument," they teased.

He made his way to one of the museums and went in to get out of the cold and to rest. Because of the weather, Michael decided to stay there until he felt it was time to look for Marlon, and he hoped that the weather wouldn't keep his friend from showing up. *Friend?*

he thought. He didn't know anything about the guy. Except, well, that. He considered backing out.

The museum closed, and Michael walked slowly to the area of the park where he planned to wait, in part because he was an hour early based on the time they had met before, but mainly because he had thought so much about what might happen that reluctance was growing. He noticed how bundled up others were as he walked, and he realized that with his heavy coat, toboggan, and scarf they might not recognize each other when they met. He brushed the snow off the bench and sat down on the cold surface to wait. He closed his eyes and stuck out his tongue to catch snowflakes like the kids from Missouri had done.

The snow on the ground muffled the sounds of the footsteps, and suddenly the bench shifted as someone sat next to him. "You better get that tongue back in your mouth; I don't want it to freeze off."

Michael turned as he recognized Marlon's voice. "Hey, Marlon. Good to see you; I was hoping you would show up here." This was Michael's first view of Marlon in daylight, and he was just as handsome as he'd imagined.

"Oh, really?" Marlon flirted. "And why's that? I wondered about you, actually. Thought I might run into you *last* week."

"Oh, I wasn't feeling well last weekend. I just hung around my room."

Marlon wasn't sure if he believed him, but he didn't let on. Rather, he got right to the point. "Listen, I want you again, but it's too fuckin' cold to be out here. How 'bout coming back to my apartment?"

"Uh, OK, I guess. How far?"

"Just a few blocks; you can make it."

Marlon pulled him up by his jacket collar. Marlon's hand so close to his chin reminded Michael of their first meeting and the way he had been pulled up that night in the darkness. He wanted their mouths to come together again, their lips to touch. His eyes closed.

"Come on, you big oaf, let's go," Marlon insisted, having already turned away, unaware of Michael's fantasy.

When they reached the apartment, they were both chilled, but in spite of this, Marlon began to undress. Michael was nervous. He had never been naked with another adult. There was the senator, of course, but that was in the dark, and the alcohol—or Michael's selective memory—kept him from recalling the image of the naked man.

Michael had seen his teammates naked, but they were boys and he had not looked at them in a sexual way. Now before him was a man, removing his clothes, one Michael knew he was about to get in bed with and whose body he would be touching and exploring. He began to undress.

As Marlon pulled his T-shirt off, Michael couldn't help but stare. He realized what a strikingly handsome figure Marlon was, with dark hair on his chest and stomach. And as Marlon lowered his pants and underwear together, the sight of his semi-erect penis and balls caused Michael to stop in mid-action as he was removing his own belt.

"What's wrong?" Marlon asked.

"Nothing," Michael replied. "It's just, well, you're beautiful. I've only seen you in the dark, and bundled up, and I didn't imagine..." His voice trailed off, and he began to blush.

"Come on." Marlon was already in the bed. He reached over and pulled Michael, still trying to remove his pants, in with him. Marlon grabbed Michael's pants legs and pulled them off, and then he did the same with his underwear. Then quickly they pulled the cover over themselves to warm up. The more experienced Marlon put his arms around Michael and pulled him close, and Michael felt Marlon's hair rub against his own chest.

"You know, I woke up the other morning dreaming of you holding me like this, your body warming me up. My dream, my thoughts, were just like this."

Michael really did have Marlon in mind as his imaginary companion when he was in the senator's bed that morning the week before, but he didn't tell Marlon where those thoughts had occurred.

Their lovemaking was much more intimate and more passionate than the quick sex they had experienced in the park. And not just for Michael, but for Marlon as well, this was a different experience. Marlon was beginning to realize that this farm boy was not like the other tricks he had enjoyed, and the thought that this could develop into a relationship flashed through his mind. Marlon quickly let the expectation of a relationship pass and decided to just enjoy the sex.

Michael, on the other hand, was not sure what to think. He allowed himself to feel the skin of a man whom he desired for the first time as he drew his hand across his partner's body. He pushed Marlon onto his back and straddled him, allowing his head to drop and his lips to meet Marlon's. He slowly lowered his body so they were pressed against each other, and then Marlon rolled them over so that he was on top of Michael. He kissed Michael on the neck and then began to move down his chest and beyond.

Their lovemaking continued for almost an hour. Marlon knew that Michael was naïve regarding sex, and he was able to introduce his partner to experiences he had never imagined. For Michael, this validated every forbidden thought and surpassed every fantasized self-pleasure of his past. He was totally immersed in the rapturous moments that led, for the first time, to a feeling of ease with his developing sexuality. Lying in bed, exhausted and naked, when he should have felt most vulnerable, he felt completely accepted and at peace. Wrapped both literally and figuratively in Marlon's strong arms, he didn't want to move. He couldn't imagine a more satisfying feeling.

Afterwards, Marlon fixed his guest a hot soda with lemon, and they sat on the bed and talked. "Confession time," Marlon told him. "Let me tell you about my name. It's not Marlon, as you know. It's

Alan. Alan Metz. A group of us use names of movie stars and such instead of our real names just for fun. Our 'Hollywood' names. As if," he laughed, but Michael noticed a resemblance to the movie star.

"I moved here from Pennsylvania after my father kicked me out of our house. He's a coal miner, and no coal miner's gonna have a fuckin' faggot for a son in this town," he said, mocking his father. "That was six years ago; I was about your age. You're about twenty, right? Anyway, I came here, got a job in a supermarket as a bag boy, and within three years was manager of the store."

"Kicked out—shit. The thought never occurred to me—I mean, with my folks. My god, I don't know what I would do." Michael began to get nervous and stood up.

"Calm down…it's OK. They aren't here; they don't know."

"I sometimes wonder about my mother. Well, my dad too. He doesn't have much to do with me, especially the last couple of years. I just think they know. Or suspect. Last night I was on the phone with them. Something wasn't right—I could tell. I wondered if they somehow knew."

Alan tried to reassure him. "You told me you had never had sex before. Unless you've said something, they couldn't know. You don't seem prissy, and you're an athlete—nothing would make them think you're a homosexual."

"That's true, I haven't had sex. I mean, before you. My mother did catch me, uh, beating off a while back, so I don't know. I mean, I'm not sure what she thought after that. But I know that's the most embarrassed I've ever felt."

Michael's feelings about himself were beginning to change as a result of this encounter, and for the first time he began to accept that he was different. He used the excuse of the cold outside, but in reality it was the feeling of security that led to him asking Alan if he could spend the night.

Four

There was anticipation among the people Michael worked with that this session of Congress would be historic. Michael had nothing to compare it to, but he had never seen so many people working so seriously, and he quickly assumed a role in Senator Bass's office. As he learned about the history of the Negro in America from associates who worked in the Senate offices, he began to realize what a different story he had learned in Tennessee. The subject of race was rarely brought up in his presence at home, and the area he lived in had no black residents. The Ku Klux Klan had originated not far to the south. His mother's sister lived with her husband between Franklin and Nashville, and she had talked about a Negro woman named Kerry who cleaned and ironed for them. But Michael never thought of that as more than any other situation where one person worked for another, and he had never met her and never thought about her family.

Ross Bass was the junior senator from his state, and he frequently sought advice or at least had discussions with Albert Gore, the senior senator. On this particular day, the two senators were scheduled to meet a group from the Southern Christian Leadership Conference. They were seeking assurance of the senators' support for the Voting

Rights Act, which would come to a vote later in the session. Michael was invited to attend and was surprised at the number of Negroes close to his age who were part of the group, and he was also surprised that they seemed to have no hesitation to speak. They treated the senators with respect, but at the same time they made their point.

An older man with them, Bayard Rustin, who spoke with an accent, seemed pleased with the younger men. Michael and Rustin exchanged glances several times during the meeting. Later Michael learned that Rustin was the assistant to Martin Luther King who had organized the march in Washington that took place a couple of years earlier. Michael had seen images of the march and heard bits of King's speech on television, but at the time it had not meant much to him. He was impressed to meet the man who had organized the march.

Senator Gore had voted against the Civil Rights Act of 1964, so his support for the current legislation could not be taken for granted. Senator Bass hadn't become a senator until later in 1964, having won a special election for the seat after the death of his predecessor, Senator Estes Kefauver, while in office. But with his origins in Pulaski, the home of the aforementioned Ku Klux Klan, he too was targeted by the Negroes seeking support.

Other important legislation was being considered, including the Elementary and Secondary Education Act and the Social Security Act of 1965, which would create Medicare and Medicaid, both of which took much of the senator's time, so when the persistent SCLC men returned for an additional meeting during the week, Senator Bass asked Michael to take care of them. Of the three young men, the one named George was tall like Michael, and like Michael, he had played high school basketball. The two hit it off and agreed to meet to shoot some baskets, although in reality neither knew how that could take place.

Michael learned that George and Isaiah, another of the Negroes, had been students at a college in Tennessee and had been on what they called Freedom Rides four years earlier that challenged segregation in parts of the South that resisted integration. On one such trip, they had been jailed for promoting equality in Mississippi and as a result had been kicked out of college. They had not sought to continue their education, instead joining Rustin's nonviolent movement to promote change.

Michael was fast learning about disparities that he had never realized existed, and he could not understand why people treated other human beings like they did. Alan had been kicked out of his home, and these men had been kicked out of school. Nothing seemed permanent—nothing seemed stable. As he learned more about Mr. Rustin and his movement, Michael began to think about how he could support it.

Michael was so involved in his work that he had little time during the day to think about Alan or their relationship. And at night he could now concentrate on his books and news magazines and studied history and current events, but by midweek he decided to read the next installment in the *Washington Post* series. Michael retrieved the folder, poured himself a glass of scotch, and began. The article had the following headline:

Those Others – III

Homosexuals Are in All Kinds of Jobs, Find Place in Many Levels of Society

The article opened with a quote that said, "The main point is that we are like anyone else except in the area of sexual orientation." The next line of the article described the speaker:

"The speaker was a well-built young man, masculine in appearance and manner."

Like me. Or Alan, Michael thought. He continued to read. *Plato? Michelangelo? Homos?* he thought to himself in astonishment.

"Homosexuals can have warm, tender feelings. Many want a stable, long-lasting relationship and search for the right male partner to share their lives."

Michael's thoughts turned to Alan. He felt comfortable with Alan and, though somewhat naïve, began to think about a future.

The article didn't really give Michael self-assurance. He only felt that when he was with Alan. The article actually made him uncomfortable because as it spoke of wanting a stable relationship, it made it seem an impossible goal. If he believed what he read, his relationship with Alan would not survive the first disagreement. And then he would be forced into the promiscuous, "highly competitive sex market" that the paper described. He learned about the high incidence of venereal disease among promiscuous homosexuals and then read this: "Society makes life difficult for any homosexual, no matter how law-abiding he is. His whole life can crumble to ruin because of exposure."

The mind works mysteriously sometimes; some people let adversity and difficulty take control, while others seek comfort and happiness. For Michael, the secure feeling he associated with Alan was beginning to dominate; Michael wanted to see Alan, and he did not want to wait until Saturday. He had not thought to get Alan's telephone number since he didn't have a phone in his room, but he did remember where he lived. It was late, however, so he decided to wait until the next night to try to find him. He poured another drink and read the entire article again. He got into bed and wrapped his arms around the spare pillow. Imagining he was with Alan, Michael fell asleep.

~

Thursday was Alan's night to go out as Marlon, but he usually didn't leave his apartment until about nine. After work, Michael ate dinner at a café near his motel, which also happened to be close to Alan's apartment, and sat for about twenty minutes longer trying to build up the nerve to go without an invitation.

While he was waiting, Alan walked in, having gotten off work an hour later than Michael. "Michael, what are you doing here?" he asked.

Michael looked up, surprised, and smiled. "I just finished dinner; I eat here quite a bit."

"I just closed the market. I eat here often too, but I guess you're usually gone by the time I get here. Working late tonight?"

"No, I finished a while ago. I've just been sitting here thinking."

"Uh-oh. Thinking about what?"

"Well, to be honest, I was going to walk to your apartment to see you. I was thinking whether I really should or not."

Alan sat down across the booth and looked Michael in the eye.

"I should have given you my telephone number. I'm usually busy on Thursday nights, but hey, why don't you come with me? I usually meet some friends at the Phoenix. It's a bar, and on Thursdays it's all men," he said, ending in a whisper.

Alan realized as he said it that he might be revealing to Michael more of his other life than he wanted. He could tell by Michael's expression that he knew exactly what Alan would be doing later that evening, and he and Michael both spoke quickly to take control of the conversation.

"That's OK—" Michael began.

Alan interrupted, "But, oh yeah, tonight I don't have to go. I mean, we can—it's up to you."

Michael had learned a little about the clubs and what went on from the articles he had read, but he wanted to hear from Alan, firsthand. "Tell me about the Phoenix. Who do you see? What do you do?"

"I usually meet a friend there, a doctor. He's in the 'Hollywood House' I told you about that I'm part of. Calls himself Dr. Casey, Ben Casey. The last two times he brought a guy who works with him at the hospital. We just talk and have drinks. There's a drag show—you know what that is? A guy performs, sings, dressed as a woman. He's, or she, is really good. She's Judy Garland!"

Then you sneak off with a guy for sex, Michael thought. But instead he said, "We can go if you want. I wouldn't mind meeting your friends. I mean, more people like us. Like me."

Michael was holding onto the hope of a relationship, that he and Alan could beat the odds against their relationship working. At the same time, Alan was thinking that maybe he had given this farm boy too much attention. He liked his body, and he enjoyed teaching the inexperienced kid how to have a good time, but he wasn't ready to give up his freedom to bang whoever he chose, as he once put it.

"Wait a minute. You aren't twenty-one are you? They card you at the door; they're real strict, especially on Thursdays. The cops watch the place like hawks. Really, I think they're watching more out of interest than duty. I mean, Doc even left with one a couple of weeks ago. I tell you what—we can't do it tonight, but I know somebody who can make you an ID; then you can get in. Why don't I call my friends and have them come over to my place? You can meet them, and then if they want to go to the club, they can go on. Now, you need to know that I told them about you."

"Told them what?" Michael asked. "That you…" He paused. "That we, uh, what we did?"

"Well, pretty much, yes. I'm sorry, but, yeah. The first night we were together, we just had sex. We didn't know each other. We always share our stories, and I told them you were a farm boy. I didn't know I would ever see you again."

"God. What are they going to want to do, for you to pass me around or something?"

"No. No, they won't. When I call him, I'll tell him that we, that I…" Alan paused for a moment before he continued. "That I'm in love," he said jokingly.

Michael felt his face turn red. The word love had not entered his mind. Relationship, yes. Love, no. This was too much. How could he be homosexual, how could he have a relationship, how could this turn into being "in love," and his parents not know? Is there some level of relationship, less than "in love" but more than just having sex regularly, that he could have with Alan that he could get away with? His mind was trying to piece all this together, and suddenly he felt at odds with himself.

"I'm just kidding you. Michael, seriously, I'm no more in love than you, so don't freak out on me. I don't know what I'm gonna tell them, but don't worry, you won't get passed around, as you say. Unless, of course, you want to," he added, half jokingly.

Michael didn't laugh.

"Can you sit here a few more minutes while I get dinner? Frances?" Alan directed his speech toward the waitress.

"Yes, hon," Frances said as she made her way to the booth.

"What's the special?"

"Meatloaf, peas, and mashed potatoes," Frances and Michael said in unison.

"He's cute," Frances said to Alan. "Where'd you land him? I'm just kidding," she said before either could answer. "I've seen you in here before. You're the Tennessee boy, working with the senator, right?"

"Yeah, that's me. Michael."

"I'll take the special. Coffee to drink," Alan said.

"I'll stay," Michael said. He thought for a moment. "If I'm going to your place, I might as well." He didn't say anything more as he stared at Alan while he ate. They paid separately and left to go to Alan's.

Alan called the doctor as soon as they got in, hoping to catch him before he left home. Dr. Casey said he would pick up his friend and they would be over in about an hour. Michael felt relaxed in Alan's apartment, and after thinking about the night he had previously spent there, he turned and asked, "Do you think we have time to go in there?" pointing toward the bedroom, unable to think of a better way to ask about sex.

"Let's go," Alan replied, not needing to think about it.

A half hour later, they lay facing each other, smiling.

"Listen, I might as well tell you something," Michael whispered.

"Oh, shit, what?"

"Oh, no big deal. You keep thinking I'm older than I am. I'm just eighteen; I won't turn nineteen until June."

"Damn, you are a young buck, aren't you," Alan laughed, remembering his comment to his friends in the club. "And fresh off the farm."

He grabbed Michael's ass. "Nice hams, too."

He pulled Michael over toward him, rolling him on his stomach, and straddled the eighteen-year-old as if to fuck him.

"Mmmmmm," Michael moaned. "Don't we need to get up?" he whispered.

"Shhhh," Alan countered. He lowered himself onto Michael, his hard penis pressed against his partner's ass. Playfully thrusting, he teased, "I guess this can wait. I don't want to spoil you, anyway, but turnabout is fair play I've always heard. Doc has never been on time in his life. Let's just lay here a bit longer."

He rolled off of Michael and pulled him close. Michael drew his fingers through Alan's hair and across his whiskered cheek.

There was a knock at the door. Alan and Michael both jumped up and quickly got dressed.

"I'm coming, I'm coming!" Alan hollered, and then he started laughing. He whispered to Michael, "That's what you were saying a while ago."

Alan let the two men in and introduced them to Michael. "Let's have a drink," he offered.

Michael and Alan may have gotten dressed, but their messed-up hair gave away what they had been doing. Doc and his friend teased them about it, but the conversation was mainly about where they worked and what they did. Alan turned the television on, and the four watched it and talked until the news came on. When Alan's friends left, he told Michael it was too late to be going home and that he would take him to work the next day.

~

When Alan was dropping Michael off at work the next morning, George and Isaiah were crossing the street on their way to the offices of some representatives. Michael called them over and introduced them to Alan. As they spoke, George noticed that Michael was wearing the same clothes he'd had on the day before.

"These guys are civil rights workers and were Freedom Riders," Michael said, hoping that Alan knew what he was talking about and would be OK with it.

Alan reached out and shook both men's hands.

"Bye, Alan, thanks for the ride," Michael said, trying to seem innocent.

As they walked toward the building, George said to Michael, "You know, Mr. Rustin's homosexual."

"What? What do you mean?"

"I mean Mr. Rustin is homosexual, and it's OK. That you are."

"Why would you say that? That I'm a homosexual?" Michael asked.

"Calm down. Now, first of all, Mr. Rustin said he thinks you are. He just seems to know these things. Second of all, I've seen homosexuals, and sometimes even I can tell. There's just something. Third, when I saw you get out of that car in those wrinkled clothes that you had on yesterday, and when you looked at that man the way you looked at him, that was a giveaway."

"Damn! Excuse me. George...Isaiah...please don't talk about this. I can't risk Senator Bass finding out."

Isaiah spoke. "Michael, we aren't here to make enemies, and we know that we need all the support we can get. We know better than to divide people because of their differences, and your difference is *no* different. Mr. Rustin has taught us that we're all human beings, and we all deserve respect, and we all deserve to live our lives as we see fit."

George broke in. "Michael, I only told you because we want you to feel comfortable. If you're acting nervous or afraid something's going to be found out, it interferes with your work—or our work if we're working together. So come on, man, don't worry."

Michael felt a little better, but he still was embarrassed.

"Just one thing," Isaiah said. "Don't think you're gonna get any of what I got," and he looked down. That really made Michael turn red, and his two Negro friends laughed.

By the next Thursday, Michael had his fake ID and was planning to meet at Alan's to go to the Phoenix. And this time when he arrived at the apartment he had an extra set of clothes, just in case he spent the night again. Around the time they were getting ready to go out, Alan received a telephone call from his doctor friend.

"Uh-huh. Oh shit. Where is he now? What's he gonna do?" was all Michael heard. When Alan hung up the phone, he said, "This is shit. Doc's technician friend, whose name is David Cochran, by the way, got picked up a while ago in the park by the police. Entrapment, that's what it is. They hang around, looking like any sexy dude, rub their piece a little to entice you, and when you speak to them, they haul you in. It's fuckin' crap. David's in jail; probably wasn't even out there trying to get anything, not this early."

"Damn," Michael said, thinking it could have been him a few weeks ago when he had sex in the park with Alan. "I would die. I would never go back to face my parents if that happened to me. What about his parents? Do they know about him?"

"I don't know. I know that he's from Virginia, not far from here, and he goes home to see them often. Other than that, I don't know. But listen, Doc still wants us to meet him at the club. He said he would fill us in on the rest there."

As they made their way to the club to meet Doc, Michael's thoughts returned to the *Post* series. He knew that part four was supposed to be about the law, but he hadn't read it yet because it made him a little nervous. The references to homosexual sex in the articles made him horny too, but he was also learning about problems and finding issues to worry about that he didn't even know were issues at all. And he just didn't really want to learn about the law and possible punishments for what he was doing. But with David taken in, Michael decided that he would read the article once he got home the next day.

At the club Doc arrived in a somber mood, and the three discussed the details, as were known, about David's plight. "Oh, he'll probably be released and just have to pay a fine, a hundred dollars or so. That will keep his name out of the papers and maybe keep him out of the park for a few weeks, but he'll just go somewhere else. The big problem comes if the police catch someone in the act, in the bushes or in a bathroom somewhere. That can land you ten years and a thousand dollars here. In some places it's worse—I think in North Carolina you can get sixty years in prison."

"Just for doing what's natural for you," Alan said. "It don't make sense. Why should anybody care what we do in private? Oh, I know, the restroom situation is public, I guess, but those laws even get you in your own home."

A man walked up and put his arm on Doc's shoulder. "Hey, good looking, what's up?"

"Not much. We were just talking about my friend David—he got busted a while ago."

"Damn. Was he really doing anything?"

"I doubt it—too early. Hey, Frank, you remember my friend Alan, and this is his honey, Michael."

"Honey?" Michael asked.

"Oh, don't be insulted," Frank said. "Good to meet you, though. Good job, Alan." Frank laughed. "Well, I'm out of here anyway; we've got a meeting tonight, trying to work out some plans for a protest that's coming up."

There was a round of good-byes, and then the conversation turned back to David. "Hey, Doc, David's about my age. Do his parents know he's one of us?" Alan asked.

"I'm not sure. I know he's on good terms with them, and he sees them quite a bit. They even came up here to see him last year when he moved into his apartment—I met them. But I don't know what they know."

It's a shame, Michael thought, *that we can't be ourselves in front of our own parents*.

No one felt like partying that evening, but Michael did spend the night at Alan's. They were intimate, but they just held each other close and didn't have sex.

~

Senators often were not in their offices on Fridays, and often the staff left early as well. Michael had lunch with some coworkers and went back to his motel after eating. He wanted to read the article about the law and did so without the help of scotch whiskey this time, a sign that he was getting used to the idea of being homosexual. Possibly.

Those Others – IV
49 States and the District Punish Overt Homosexual Acts as Crimes

The article confirmed what Doc had said about the punishments, that it ranged from a "minimum one-year prison sentence to North Carolina's maximum of 60 years."

Michael thought about having to spend the rest of his life in prison. *Stay out of North Carolina*, he promised himself.

He read what a U.S. district judge wrote ordering a new trial after a man was sentenced to twenty to thirty years:

> Is it not time to redraft a criminal statute first enacted in 1533? And if so, cannot the criminal law draftsmen be helped by those best informed on the subject—medical doctors—in attempting to classify offenders? Is there any public purpose served by a possible 60-year maximum or even a 5-year minimum imprisonment of the occasional or one-time homosexual, without treatment, and if so, what is it?

Michael thought about his Negro friends and how they were fighting to overturn laws that treated them as second-class citizens, and here were laws that made him a criminal. *All these laws*, he thought, *are so archaic. People are people, whether* Negro *or white, and whether heterosexual or homosexual. Yet laws like these, whether they divide people into groups which become classes, like the segregation laws, or laws which criminalize behavior, just seem in their true purpose to put the majority of people, the heterosexual white people, in control.*

He read of homosexuals being hounded by the police and of peepholes being used by police for surveillance, and he wondered if he was being watched when he went to the club.

Michael also read about differing religious views:

> "Towards a Quaker View of Sex," a statement prepared by a group of British Quakers in 1963, suggested that society "should no more deplore homosexuality than left-handedness," although it can prohibit certain types of behavior.

Michael's family was not very religious, but certainly the Methodist church he had sometimes attended as a child with his mother would not agree with the tolerant view put forth by these Quakers just two years ago. Michael had not considered the religious implications of his actions, and he couldn't, in fact, even decide if such considerations mattered. Later he would realize they did.

In spite of what he learned from Doc and the article, he felt somewhat relieved to read that the Washington police were working with the homosexual community and a group called the Mattachine Society so that blackmail attempts could be reported without fear of prosecution for those doing the reporting.

This article ended with a note stating, "*Next: Jobs and security for the homosexual.*"

He decided to wait until Saturday or Sunday to read the final article. He had enough new knowledge to digest at one sitting.

~

The next day was Saturday, and Michael visited the Smithsonian Institution, which took practically the whole day. Alan's Saturdays were spent at work, so Michael wasn't able to spend time with his honey, a term he now used to describe Alan after initially being embarrassed by it. Michael simply continued his routine of Saturday sightseeing. Late in the afternoon, he went back to the motel to rest, and since he had the time, Michael decided he would read the final article. Michael was also intrigued by the article because he had a concern about his own job.

Those Others – V
Homosexual's Militancy Reflected in Attacks on Ouster from U.S. Jobs

> When a public hearing on job discrimination was held in Washington two years ago, the Mattachine Society submitted a statement protesting discrimination against homosexuals in both public and private employment.
>
> The homosexual pictures himself as a member of a true minority group suffering unreasonable discrimination and social prejudice.
>
> His situation, he says, is even worse than that of the Negro because he has to fight the active hostility of the Federal Government. Among his complaints are these:
>
> He can't hold a government job. He can't get security clearance. He can't serve his country in the armed forces. His choice, as he sees it, is either to lie or to be an outcast in society with neither the duties nor the rights of other citizens.

Wait, he thought, *now they're talking about me. Not just what I might do with my lover, but what I might want to do with my life*. Michael continued reading the article.

> But today society offers no place, no help, and no hope to the homosexual. Laws are harsh on him; his existence is precarious; exposure brings ruin and social ostracism.
>
> Yet society has to deal with the homosexual in its midst. And it will never be able to do this with fairness and compassion until it understands more about what has been called "the riddle of homosexuality."

To Michael, a riddle was a question with a surprising and often funny answer. He had certainly been surprised at his life lately, but he didn't consider his life a joke. What the *Post* had considered a "riddle" it also described as a "problem." And rather than answering the riddle, this final segment of the series created more questions for him. Was it worth it to try to continue this homosexual life? Was he just doing this because he was away from home? Would he be living like this if he were still in Franklin, or even in Nashville?

The comparison of the homosexual's problems to the Negro's problems made him want to talk with Mr. Rustin, who was both a homosexual and a Negro. And his developing interest in government and history as a career now had to be considered with serious thoughts about his sexual preference and the impact that could have on his future.

Five

During the next month, Michael continued his work in Senator Bass's office as well as his relationship with Alan. He learned from Alan that the home he was kicked out of was a racially prejudiced home. Alan's father had moved from West Virginia after losing his job at a coal mine there because of racial incidents. He had found a similar mining job in a town in Pennsylvania that did not have a population of Negroes—that way, he wouldn't be forced to work side by side with them.

Alan seemed at ease with black people, but Michael realized that both of them had some degree of prejudice. The difference was that Alan's prejudice seemed to result from what he had been taught, whereas Michael's seemed to stem from what he had not learned. Alan had heard negativity regarding Negroes as a child and grew up believing that blacks were less than equal. Michael, on the other hand, had not been taught, at home or at school, the full story of Negroes and their struggle, so what seemed to some to be a disrespect of Negroes stemmed from a lack of knowledge.

They talked almost every day about issues regarding race, and if not that, issues regarding homosexuality. Michael explained that he had limited experience with people who were Negroes and had not learned overt bigotry because there were no black people in his town—there was no lunch counter for white people to keep the Negroes away from, there was no bus service to demand up-front seating for whites, and there were no public water fountains from which "coloreds" could be denied access. Alan, on the other hand, had seen his father come home bloodied from fights and had been taught that his father's views were right. But Alan had watched the news, and as he was dealing with the consequences of his homosexuality and being thrown out of his own home, he equated that injustice with that of treating Negroes differently because of their race. As a result, his views moderated.

Michael seemed to think that if he had been raised where Negroes were present, that he could have been a friend to their community, but there was no way to know for sure. But it did make him feel better to say it. And it seemed to bolster his growing belief that people should treat homosexuals with respect, whether they knew any or not. He had begun to think that homosexuals were common enough that everyone knew at least one or two—they just might not know of their preferences.

Michael and Alan talked about living together, and this was tough for both of them. Even though Michael was making pretty good money by now, his parents were still paying for his motel room, and they would welcome the relief if they didn't have to send him money each week. He wondered what they would think if he moved in with another man. He considered not telling them and using the money to reimburse Alan for expenses. With his pay from the senator's office, he could afford to do that without directly lying to his parents. He also remembered the article in the *Post* saying "society pressures tend to break up the homosexual couple" and that line about not surviving the first disagreement. He wondered what others in town who did not know his secret would think if he moved into Alan's apartment. George had known from the way he and Alan looked at one another. Would it be that obvious to others?

Michael learned that Alan had a sense of sexual freedom far different from his own. Michael was just beginning to accept his own sexuality, and that was freedom enough for him. If he wanted to consider it a form of rebellion, just desiring sex with men and acting on his desires with one man was rebellion enough. Alan, on the other hand, had accepted his homosexuality for ten years or so. After catching Alan and his cousin in the act in their garage, Alan's father had pushed him out the door when he was a junior in high school.

Alan had managed to live on the street and in a friend's house in order to finish high school. But while living on the street, in order to make money for food, he began to hustle around town, providing services for a variety of men ranging from coal miners to a pharmacist and a conservative pastor. It could be that the men knew his story and knew to come to him, but Alan liked to think it was he who recognized the desires of his customers, and in doing so, he developed a good sense of recognizing who was really homosexual and who was not, a skill that had kept him out of jail as the years went on.

By the time Alan met Michael, he was no longer making money off sex, but his desire for frequent sex continued. In spite of being used by the men in his hometown, he always felt a sense of satisfaction from sex apart from the immediate gratification. This stemmed from his feeling that in doing so he was getting back at his father.

When he moved to Washington and began to make money legitimately, he realized he didn't have to depend on payment for sex for his living expenses and he could become more choosy about with whom he had sex. The men he had provided for in the past were, for the most part, older and not in the best physical shape. His priorities changed from men who could afford to pay to men who were his age or younger and in good shape, and in Washington, DC, there was no shortage of good-looking young men cruising for sex.

All of this was revealed to Michael during a discussion they had about living together. It started with Michael asking about Alan's parents and how they found out he was homosexual and how it resulted in his getting kicked out of his home.

"Do you really want to hear that?" Alan asked. "I mean, here I'm in our garage. My dad had put some weights and a bench out there for me to train on. I was about sixteen or seventeen, and my cousin and I were working out. He was a hunk, let me tell you. I was benching, he was spotting me, and damn, he was standing right up by my head and I could see right up his gym shorts. He was older than me, about nineteen or so—I guess around your age. Anyway, I could see his balls, and I closed my eyes. Should have been concentrating on bench pressing, but in my mind I saw the rest of his meat, and I began to get hard. I mean, we were both just wearing our gym shorts, and it was pretty obvious. He noticed. Anyway, I pretended to be having some difficulty with the weights, and he grabbed the bar and helped me return it to the stand. Then he came around and straddled the bench and me and said he thought we'd had enough of that. I could tell what he wanted, and I grabbed his shorts and made him step forward and pulled them down. Well, you can imagine what was going on from here, but just about a minute later my father walked in.

"He charged over to where we were, saying, 'What the fuck is going on?' He pushed my cousin off of me, and as I was trying to sit up, he swung at me and knocked me down. He kicked me, and my cousin got up and pushed him away. My cousin is a moose, and he told my father that if he let it out what we were doing, he would live to regret it. They yelled back and forth while I lay there bleeding, and finally he told me to get my shit and get out, that no fuckin' faggot was going to live in his house. I got what little I had and left and haven't seen him since."

"Holy cow," Michael responded. "Really, you never talked to him about it, never got to explain?"

"What's to explain? In his eyes, I'm a damn faggot sucking my cousin off, and that's all there is to it. And with his temper, remember, it got him in trouble with the Negroes. No telling what he said to them to get them riled up. I guess he just thinks that since he got beat up by people teaching him a lesson that he can teach me a lesson in the same way. It's all he knows."

"Shoot, Alan, I'm sorry. I had no idea you had it so rough."

"Listen, don't feel sorry for me. I mean, things are good for me now. I make a good living, and I live how I want to live."

"Well, does living how you want to live include living with me? I mean, me moving in here with you?" Michael asked.

On one hand, Michael was everything Alan could ask for physically, and they got along really well, and the thought of living with Michael had crossed his mind on several occasions. On the other hand, Alan was not sure he was ready to give up his sexual freedom.

And Michael was naïve if he thought Alan could give up sex with strangers just like that. In spite of what Michael had read about cruising and anonymous sex in the articles, he didn't understand the culture of homosexuality that Alan was coming from. He expected Alan to be able to turn off his desire for anyone but him. It was an unrealistic expectation, perhaps, but after knowing each for less than two months, they decided to live together.

Michael did not know any other male couples who lived together, and he had no role models or standards to work toward, but they both agreed that the time they spent together was better than the time they spent apart. So at the end of a paid-up week at the motel, Michael gathered his belongings into a suitcase and a laundry bag and checked out of the room that had been his home since the first week of the year.

∾

Work for Michael became routine, and he helped the rest of the staff deal with the increasing numbers of letters the office received. Senator Bass was more interested in the Social Security legislation that was being prepared than the voting bill, but the public was more interested in the latter, it seemed. The senator had a prepared response that Michael and the others sent in reply to the majority of the constituents, but every once in a while a letter would arrive that required the senator's personal attention. In these cases Michael was amazed at the senator's ability to write a calming response to a hateful letter without really answering the writer's question.

George and Isaiah became less frequent visitors as Senators Bass and Gore's position on the voting bill strengthened, and they spent much of their time visiting the nine House representatives from Tennessee. So Michael was not aware of their plans to attend the march from Selma to Montgomery scheduled for March 7 until the Thursday before the event, the day they were planning to leave.

"Oh, I don't know, a few hundred, mostly from Alabama. We know there will be some folks from Georgia and Mississippi as well. Might as well add Tennessee!"

"Do you all feel safe, driving there? After all that's happened?" Michael asked. "How long will it take you to get there?"

"We're driving to Nashville tonight. We're going to stay at a pastor's house we know from school. We'll leave Saturday and drive down through north Alabama, which won't be as risky, I think, as driving from Atlanta. We don't have very good memories of that route."

"So you'll be activists as well as trying to influence politicians, huh?"

"You forget, we're already activists, remember? We were Freedom Riders and have been in jail in Mississippi, so the threat of jail doesn't intimidate us."

"Now, explain to me why Selma, Alabama? Of all places?"

George told him that he had been in the congregation on January 2, which happened to be the day Michael had arrived in Washington, when Dr. King spoke at Brown Chapel in defiance of an injunction against promoting civil rights. He pulled a piece of paper from his wallet where a passage from Dr. Martin Luther King Jr.'s sermon was written and handed it to Michael to read. The paper told how that day marked the beginning of a concerted effort to get the vote.

"He told us that the pace was too slow, and that it would take us one hundred and five years at the rate we were going to register all the voters who were qualified," George continued. "And that the campaign to get voting rights was beginning that day. But he also said that if that campaign failed, we would appeal to Congress. That's what Dr. King told us that day. I carry it with me for inspiration and courage. We are part of that campaign. That's why we work the street, and that's why we work the halls of Congress.

"Here's something else I got that day," George said, pulling another piece of paper from his billfold. "You can have it."

He handed the folded paper to Michael, who read the hand-typed words aloud: "I sought my soul, but my soul I could not see; I sought my God, but my God eluded me. I sought my vote, and I found all three."

"That's a handbill that the people there were passing out to spread their message," George explained.

"Goodness. You're being part of history, you know. But listen, y'all just be careful and get back here and tell me about it," Michael replied as he refolded the piece of paper and put it in his billfold.

~

On Sunday evening, Michael and Alan were in the apartment watching television when the news came on. Local and Alabama state police had attacked a crowd of about six hundred civil rights workers in Selma, Alabama. The scenes flashed on the screen of brutal attacks near the Edmund Pettus Bridge, on the outskirts of Selma, which the marchers were to cross on their way to Montgomery. The group had not even made it out of town. They saw black-and-white images of bloody marchers and strained to see if they could identify George and Isaiah, but with the grainy picture on Alan's old TV, they couldn't. It was one thing to overcome the threat of being jailed, Michael thought. But Michael had not seriously considered the threat of violence.

There was no way to get in touch with his friends, and he would just have to wait until news came through the Senate office or the next day's newspaper. Michael's awareness of the violence associated with the civil rights movement had grown over the past two months, but now it was hitting close to home. These two men were his friends. And they were the only two people, outside of other homosexuals, who knew of his secret.

Monday one of the staff members from another senator's office reported that Isaiah had been injured, somewhat seriously, and George had escaped injury altogether. He also reported that another attempt at the march would be made the next day, and George would stay and participate in it. Isaiah was staying with a family in Selma. Michael urged the staff member to keep him posted of any updates.

Michael also kept up with what was going on by watching the evening news on television and by reading the newspaper. He learned that a court had ordered that the march could not take place. In spite of this, by Tuesday about twenty-five hundred people had gathered. King and other leaders had decided not to march against the court order, so he turned it around soon after the march began, to the disappointment of those who had come to take part. But King was confident that the federal judge who was reviewing the order would rule in favor of letting a march take place, and he thought that waiting until there was federal blessing on the protest was a better strategy than another confrontation.

That evening, however, three white ministers were beaten with clubs in an area of Selma that supported segregation. One of the men, James Reeb, was seriously injured and was taken to Selma Hospital, where he was turned away. Reeb was transported to Birmingham's University Hospital, where he died two days later. George had gone with Reeb to Birmingham, offering support and thanks to the injured man and his wife, whom he met at the hospital.

Michael had no way of knowing that George had accompanied Reeb. He only knew of the minister's injury and was caught off guard when a call came to the senator's office for him from Birmingham.

"I don't know anyone in Birmingham," he told the secretary as she directed him to the telephone, but he did know that his friends were still in Alabama.

"Hello," he answered nervously.

He was relieved when he heard George speak. George told him that Reverend Reeb had died. He was calling Michael, he told him, because he needed to talk to someone, and Michael would be less worried than Isaiah or his family.

"George, I do worry. I've been trying to keep up, and the TV and newspapers keep me informed, but I haven't heard anything about you for days. I thought you were still in Selma or back in Nashville. Get back up here; it's too dangerous down there."

"I'm fine, and I'm safe. I've just never seen a man die before. If I had called my family, they would have worried too much. But I just wanted to touch base and let you know why I wasn't back yet."

George returned to Tennessee and was back in Washington by the time Judge Frank Johnson issued his ruling in favor of the SCLC to allow the march to take place. King immediately announced that the march would take place on March 21, and when George learned of this, he told Michael that he would be returning to Selma for that attempt.

"We just have to keep up the pressure. We can't back down, or justice will never be delivered," he said.

Isaiah had returned to Nashville so that his injuries could heal, and it was unsure if he would be returning or not.

~

The next morning Michael sent word that he wanted to talk with George, and that afternoon the two met.

"Alan and I talked a lot last night; we stayed up late. Listen, we both have decided that we want to go with you to Selma. We understand that we need rights as well, as homosexuals, and we feel that we can't ask society to recognize us without discrimination if we aren't willing to fight for your rights as well. I already spoke with Senator Bass, and—well, that's another story. He thinks my parents will be really upset, but he did give me the time off to go. Alan is the manager at the market, and he said he wouldn't have any trouble taking a few days off."

"Are you serious? Do you know what kind of trouble you could get into, riding with a Negro through Alabama? Have you ever been to anything like this?"

"I know. We talked about that. But to make change happen, there has to be risk involved. We're willing to take that risk. Besides, I need to do this with Alan by my side. We'll both be by your side, too. Isaiah, too, if he's up to it by then."

"OK, but you saw what happened to that white preacher, and he's dead now. And you don't know the half of it, what went on that day.

"We marched from Brown Chapel toward the bridge, hundreds of us. The bridge has a rise in it, and as we began to climb that rise, it was as if we were marching toward heaven. We truly thought we were on our way.

"But as we topped the rise, that's when we saw them. The police were at the foot of the bridge on the other side. But we kept marching, and as we got closer, we could see they had clubs. We stopped, and they ordered us back, but then we started marching and marched right into them. That's when it started—the beatings, the tear gas. Some of them were on horses, just walking over people who were down. It was awful.

"Once they saw that we were retreating, they increased their intensity. I mean, they were like rabid dogs. We ran back to the church, and some of us made it, but some of us didn't. But they chased us into the church, even riding their horses up the stairs and almost into the building.

"They were shooting into the homes nearby to keep people inside. They were yelling, 'Get the hell out of town! We want all niggers off the streets.' People were hurt, lying on the ground, and they wouldn't even let others come out and tend to them. That's how Isaiah got hurt, trying to help somebody. He got knocked down and stepped on by a horse.

"Now, we don't expect that kind of reception this time, but we didn't expect it that day, either. But if you're sure you want to join us, we would welcome you," George concluded.

"We need to do this," Michael responded. "With you."

"Well, you can change your mind at any time until we leave Nashville, I guess." He took Michael's hand. "Michael, we are brothers," he said, and he pulled him close and hugged him.

Discussing the issue of race and their pasts brought Alan and Michael closer, and the discussion that led to the decision to march with the Negroes was an indication that they could approach tough issues together and work their way through them. Alan had seen the results of racial violence firsthand with his father and at first accused Michael of having lofty ideals that were influencing him without weighing all of the risks. But Michael's open mind was a result of reading and study, combined with a portion of naïveté. Plus he remembered the line from the *Post* article that said the situation for homosexuals "is even worse than that of the Negro." Michael wasn't sure he agreed with that, but he did feel that both groups needed to work for each other. The important thing, as far as Michael was concerned, was that he and Alan had reached a conclusion and made a decision together. He was glad to have avoided the type of disagreement that the newspaper reported a homosexual relationship would not survive.

Michael's big decision was whether to tell his mother and father that he was going. Senator Bass was leaving that up to him. Michael was already hiding from them the fact that he was living with Alan. He sought the advice of David, the recently jailed technician who seemed to have a good relationship with his parents. Although Michael was not planning to tell his parents the secret of his sexuality, he thought David's experience in broaching difficult subjects with his parents, if true, could help him. He arranged to meet David on Saturday afternoon along the mall, close to the Washington monument.

It was a sunny afternoon, a perfect early spring day. Tourists were crowding the mall, and there was a line at the Washington Monument. In spite of the stark contrast in the weather, Michael was reminded of the day he had accompanied the grade school children to the top and how they teased him about his height. They made sure to remain in the open, at David's suggestion, so that no one could accuse them of meeting for "immoral purposes."

"David, I just want to ask you outright, do your parents know you're homosexual?" Michael asked.

"Why are you asking that? What is it to you?"

"I thought that my parents were pretty normal, typical, but since living here, I'm not that sure. I'm trying to decide whether to let them in on something."

"That you're homosexual?" David was surprised. He knew Michael was becoming more accepting of his sexuality and that he wanted to work in some way for equality, but David assumed that it was most likely without his parents' knowledge.

"No, not that. No, Alan and I are going—well, we're going to Selma, Alabama, to march to Montgomery with the Negroes and the SCLC. I have to decide if I should tell my mother and father. I'm not sure how to bring up a tender subject like that, and I thought that if you had spoken to your parents about being homosexual, then you could give me some tips."

"My parents know I'm 'gay,' a homo. But it's not because I sat them down to make an announcement. You know, I'm a little more, uh, swishy, I guess than you. They knew. Said they knew from when I was a kid."

"You're not girlish or sissy by any means, David."

"Well, I know, but compared to my brothers, there's a difference, and my parents noticed it. When I went to college, by chance my roommate was gay too, and throughout college we became a couple, I guess. Once he came home with me—well, he came home with me lots—but one time my dad heard us fooling around, and he just told us we should keep what we do in private, not to dare let my mother see that, and went on about his business. We've never really discussed it."

David thought for a moment. "Well, I take that back. We did discuss it once. A local guy everybody knew was queer got arrested, and they decided it was time to have a talk with me. Both of them, they brought it up, not me. God, I was embarrassed—in front of my mother, talking about my preference of having sex with men. But I was able to convince them, whether it was true or not, that I don't put myself in the type of situations that lead to arrest. Ha! That's a joke now, huh? Anyway, they don't even know I got picked up here. I paid the fine, and it's pretty much erased from public record. But only because I knew the desk sergeant and gave him a blow job. And by the way, he blew me too. But aside from that, I don't think I can be of much help to you."

"I don't know, I've really not been one to hide things from them—not till I moved here and started seeing Alan, anyway," Michael said. "I can't imagine my father being that nonchalant about it, though. I mean, you've got great parents. Alan's dad beat his ass and kicked him out. And mine, I just don't know."

"Well, from several friends' experiences I can tell you it's never simple, and you never know how they'll react. They could be as loving as you could believe and then show nothing but hatred and fear if you tell them—about homosexuality, that is—or they could be distant or live-and-let-live sorts like mine and be real accepting. Now you're dealing with issues of race and possibly putting yourself in danger. So how do they feel about race? That's what you need to consider."

"We didn't have any Negroes in the area where I come from. We rarely saw them. It was never discussed, so I don't know. My mom, now, is a Methodist, or was, and I know they've been pretty supportive of the civil rights movement, but that doesn't mean she would be supportive of my involvement. It's just hard to know."

"Well, I hope you decide that you can tell them and that it turns out good for you because there's nothing better than having parents support you in what you do. And in who you are. Poor Alan—his dad would really shit if he knew he was going on that march. Wow."

"Yeah, you know it really tears him up about his father. He doesn't talk much about it, but I know that it does. I think part of his reason for agreeing to go is because he knows his father would be against it. Don't tell him I said that, please?"

"Oh, I won't. I don't talk to him about his family. Only if he brings it up."

Michael told David about his experience with the kids and talked him into riding up to the top of the monument. They looked out over the mall toward the Capitol.

"You know," David said in a low voice so as not to be overheard, "you really have done a number on Alan. I think he would do anything you asked him to."

Michael strained to spot the bench where he had first encountered Alan. "No, we discussed this trip at length. We went over the positives as they related to me and the negatives as they related to me, and then we did the same for him. I didn't try to influence him, and he didn't influence me. We both decided for our own reasons that this trip was what we needed to do. If his reason is to prove something about his father, fine. Mine is because it's what I feel we need to do if we expect others to help us. I mean, it's just the right thing, and it's the way it works."

"You've become quite the little militant homo, haven't you?" David laughed.

Six

Michael lay down in the front seat and covered himself with a blanket.

"I'm not taking any chance," he said, "of my mother or father seeing me. Our house is just a few miles from here, and they could be on the way to the store or somewhere and see us."

George, riding alone in the backseat, couldn't help but laugh. Michael was tall and muscular, and it seemed odd that he would be afraid of being seen. Alan was driving George's car and didn't mind Michael resting his head in his lap as they drove through town.

"So this is home. Not much to it, it seems," Alan said.

Michael rose up to peek out the window. "Our house is about a mile and a half up that way. I went to school right over there," he said without pointing, and then he quickly lowered his head.

George's car had the best chance of making the trip without any mechanical trouble, so they brought it. Besides, they decided, Alan's DC license plates would arouse suspicion. They had driven to Nashville the day before and spent the night at the home of some friends of George and Isaiah's from their days in college. Isaiah was almost recovered, but knew he wouldn't be able to make the walk, so he didn't go.

Michael and George finally had the chance to shoot some basketball the afternoon before they left Nashville. Alan wasn't interested, so the two of them walked a block away to a small park where there was a basketball goal. The neighborhood was in a section of town where blacks lived, and Michael stood out. There were some younger kids on some swings and a babysitter who was, they assumed, watching both the kids and the basketball players.

"I've got a question for you," George began. "Don't get mad or anything, but why would you choose that?"

"Choose what?" Michael asked.

"Choose to be queer. Look over there. Why would you give up that—if she was a white girl, I mean—for your own kind?"

"I don't think I chose this. I didn't date much in school—I mean, I just wasn't interested. What with basketball and homework, who had the time? Anyway, the thought of being with a man never crossed my mind, really, until I moved away from home."

"So what happened in DC that made you want to be with a man?"

Michael didn't want to tell him how he and Alan met, but it wasn't really a lie when he replied, "I don't know."

They were playing a game of H-O-R-S-E, and Michael was winning; he had just two misses, H-O to George's three, H-O-R. "You know, I guess I'm just kidding myself. Of course I thought about men, but I didn't really know what two men would do together, just like you probably wondered what you would do with a girl when you were younger. But I knew I had a different feeling when I thought of a man than I did when I thought of a woman. In fact, there wasn't a feeling when I thought of a woman."

"I wonder why that is?" George asked. "I've asked Mr. Rustin about it too, and he couldn't really answer. But you know, if I didn't know him and have such respect for him in spite of his homosexuality, I probably wouldn't be here talking to you about it."

"I'm hoping to get to talk with him about it. Is he pretty agreeable? I mean, to talk to?"

"Yeah, once he gets to know you and realizes you aren't out to get him or make fun or anything. With what he knows—or thinks he knows—about you, I'm sure he would talk with you."

H-O-R-S-E for Michael. George had come back strong and won, probably because he was trying to impress the babysitter.

They played some more as they continued to talk. "Maybe we'll run into him down in Alabama," Michael said.

"Probably. I know he'll be speaking. At least, he plans to."

"So what about you?" Michael asked. "I've never seen you with a girl. You're asking me these questions. Are you wondering about this yourself?" Michael asked as he pointed at his crotch. He couldn't believe he had just asked George that, probably because he was upset that he had lost the game. He felt himself turn red.

George hurled the basketball at him. "Fuck, no," he shot back. *Well, yeah, but I can't tell you.*

George had considered what sex with a man would be like. One of the Freedom Riders he had travelled with was homosexual and had made advances while seated next to George on a bus one night. George had ignored the advance, pretending to be asleep, and nothing happened. Since that time he had danced around the issue, trying to obtain information without admitting to others or himself why. He had peppered Rustin with questions, but always in a way that put the emphasis on his mentor, not on himself. His friend Isaiah had seemed a little less comfortable around Rustin after learning he was homosexual, and George certainly didn't want him finding out.

"I just don't have a girlfriend now because I spend so much time on the road between here and DC, and our work is so involved I just haven't had the time. I'm OK, though."

Since the night on the bus, George had been with several women and didn't consider himself to be homosexual. If he had been familiar with the Kinsey Report, he might have understood himself to be a person who could be comfortable with either a male or a female, but instead there was just a curiosity there. That curiosity is what led him to begin the conversation with "why would you choose that?"

"Someday I'll meet someone, and she'll be the right person for me; I'm just not in any big hurry."

Michael had seen George looking at the babysitter throughout the game, and he did not doubt what he had been told.

The route they chose was part interstate and part four-lane or two-lane highway. Not far into Alabama the interstate ended, and they took Highway 31 through Athens and into Decatur, where they made their first stop to use the restroom and buy soft drinks. The man behind the counter looked at them suspiciously, but George assured them it was a safe place to stop.

With Alan driving the entire time, Michael riding shotgun, and George in the backseat so as not to appear "out of order," they bypassed Cullman, which was known for its bigotry and was reputed to have signs at its borders warning Negroes to be out of the city by sundown. In Birmingham they didn't stop because even though Bull Conner, the racist public safety commissioner, was no longer in office, his attitudes were still commonplace. They drove on to Bessemer before stopping for gas.

They carried lunch that was prepared by their hosts in a red and white metal cooler in the trunk: fried chicken, potato salad, homemade rolls, and colas. Roadside parks were plentiful, but having knowledge of ambushes at such parks, they decided not to chance stopping. They retrieved their lunch while parked at the service station and ate on the road.

Their next stop was at a service station south of Maplesville, owned by an older, gray-haired Negro named Will who walked with a limp. George knew the safe service stations along the route; he had a list of places they could stop that were known to be friendly. George and Isaiah had stopped at Will's earlier in the month; the gas station owner told them he wasn't surprised to see George coming back through, and he asked George where his friend was. He said that business had been good that day and the day before, and he thought they would have a good crowd in Selma, which wasn't far away.

Before they left, Will pulled Michael and Alan aside and spoke to them in language they could hardly understand. "What chu are doin' is goin' a make Alabama a bettuh place fo' my granddaughtuh. It's 'cause of white peoples like you boys and white men like dose in Congress dat we can make dis happen. Not da march, I means, but de laws bein' passed in Congress an signed by Pres'dent Johnson."

He took two new pennies, dated 1965, out of his pocket and handed one to each.

"Keep dese in your wallet, and if'n you hab doubts 'bout what's goin' on, pull it out. It has Abra'm Lincoln on da front. My grandpaw was livin' when Pres'dent Lincoln freed his famly. He b'longed to an ownuh whose place watun far from 'ere, jes over dat rise. If'n you get in trouble, take dat penny out and r'membuh what Lincoln did, and know dat you are jest followin' up on what he a started. Someday dey'll make some money wit Johnson on it, fo' what he's a doin'.

"But Pres'dent Lincoln is da one. One time he said, 'Whate'er you are, be a good one.' Dat's what my daddy tol' me, too. Simple words, but strong."

While Will was talking, Michael noticed a wide-eyed little girl with hair sticking up in little poufs, seven or eight years old, in the gas station, peeking out over the windowsill. He smiled and gave a little wave, and she immediately ducked down. A moment later she rose back up, brought her hand up close to her face, and weakly waved back. Then she was gone again.

At thirty-one cents a gallon, their fourteen gallons came to $4.34. George took a five-dollar bill out of an envelope to hand the man. He refused, telling them he couldn't leave his business and didn't think he could walk the distance anyway, but that he had made enough money the past two days to let them go without paying.

"Dat'll be my contribushun t'your effort," he said.

They could tell the old man was close to tears.

"Jest be careful; we'll all be a prayin' for you."

Michael was touched by Will's story of his grandfather. To know someone whose ancestor was actually a slave impressed him. The fact that Will had lived with and learned from a slave astounded him. The penny, a gift from the poor black man, seemed to come from a different era even though it was shiny and new. He took it and wrapped it in the folded handbill that George had given him and placed it in his billfold. In doing so, he made the connection between the era of slavery and the fight that Martin Luther King was leading.

They were quiet in the car until they got close to Selma, where George turned and said, "Remember Bull Connor we told you about? In Birmingham? He was born right here. Selma, Alabama. All that hatred comes from right here. He took it to Montgomery and then to Birmingham. And in some ways, he's partly responsible for us being here today. Thank you, Bull, for helping us to realize we need to change things. Right, Michael?"

"Yeah," Michael said mindlessly. His mind was elsewhere. He was thinking about the trip. What would his friends in Franklin have thought had they seen him riding in the car with a Negro to a protest in Selma, Alabama? They certainly would have been surprised. What would they think of Alan? What about the man in Decatur? The area where they stopped had both black and white people milling around, so was it unusual for them to see blacks and whites travelling together? The service station owner hadn't said anything; however, he did stare. But then again, George's list had directed them there, so it was probably OK. In Bessemer they were eyed suspiciously also. Was this because they were so close to Birmingham, where everybody, black or white, had reason to be wary, it seemed? And in Maplesville, what about the little black girl? Had she ever seen a white man before? He thought back to when he was her age, and he didn't think he had seen a black person, so maybe not. What was she thinking when she saw her grandfather talking to two white men? He thought she might be missing something, not knowing white people. Then he realized he might have missed out, too, not knowing black people as he was growing up. He looked at Alan, who was looking out the opposite window, and wondered what he was thinking about all of this.

"The bridge is straight ahead, but we're going to Brown Chapel to meet the folks we're staying with," George said as they turned left off the highway. They pulled up to the church, and Michael was in awe. The colorful, grand structure with its two towers and the round window over the three arches at the top of the stairs looked nothing like the black-and-white image of the church he had seen on television. There were people in the parking lot, mostly Negroes, and while George spoke with several, Michael and Alan leaned up against the car and Alan smoked a cigarette.

A group of men came out of the church, and as they were coming down the stairs, Michael recognized Bayard Rustin. Michael recalled meeting him in the Senate building. "That's Bayard Rustin—remember, I told you that George said he was homosexual. Everybody knows, yet here he is helping to lead this effort, and there's no problem."

"Which one?" Alan asked.

"To the left, with the black glasses," Michael said as Rustin recognized him and waved. He walked over and spoke, and Michael reintroduced himself and Alan.

"I hope to get to talk with you over the next few days," Michael said.

"There will be plenty of time for that," Rustin replied, and he excused himself.

"Where's he from?" Alan asked after Rustin left. "That accent."

"I don't know. Maybe Canada. Sort of sounds British, doesn't he? Very formal."

They would later learn that Rustin was born in West Chester, Pennsylvania, and that would give him and Alan something to talk about. They also learned that his accent was developed purposely. His favorite teacher, Maria Brock, spoke eloquently, and she influenced him to speak in a more refined manner, with an upper-class British accent of sorts. His speaking skills were well-developed by the time he graduated from high school. He won an award for public speaking—the first black student in his integrated high school to do so—and he was chosen to speak at graduation.

George brought over the man and woman who were to be their hosts for the evening. After introductions, they returned to their cars and headed to the couple's home.

Michael and Alan were given a bed in the spare room to sleep on, although the host couple did not know they were lovers. George slept on a pallet of blankets and quilts on the living room floor. Michael was glad to be able to rest after such an eventful day.

"This is so strange," Michael whispered to Alan as they closed the door to the room.

"Why? What do you mean?"

"This bed. I mean, the quilts on it. At home, on cold nights, I slept under quilts like these that my grandmother had made. I bet you that these were made by this family."

"Well, they're nice, that's for sure. They should keep us warm."

"A lot of love goes into these quilts. I remember when I was little watching my granny and mom work on quilts. I wanted to help, so they let me cut some squares. I tried to sew, but my stitchin' wasn't too good.

"This one, the one on top, the pattern is called Blackford's Beauty, and I had one just like it. Well, different colors, of course, but the same design. My granny said her granny made that quilt up where they came from in East Tennessee. And here's one like it in Selma, Alabama."

"You, going all crazy about quilts! You crack me up."

"Well, it just reminds me of home—my parents' house. I don't know about the rest. Those patterns are really different, unlike any I've seen. But whoever made them sure did a good job. Look at the edges, how this border is sewn. And you just wait, you'll be warm tonight."

"That's because I'll have you right up against me," Alan replied, a little too loudly.

"Shhh," Michael responded. "Come on, let's see."

They stripped to their underwear and T-shirts and crawled into bed, both from the same side.

"I'm not warm yet," Alan complained.

"You will be. But aren't you glad to finally be able to lie down? I'm beat, aren't you?"

"Yeah, me too," Alan replied.

"Well, what do you think? About all this?" Michael asked.

"You know, I've seen what can happen when tempers flare. I saw my father come home bloodied and beaten by Negroes. Sure, he had it coming, but these people, the people we have met today, I don't think they would lift a club. They're different than the people who beat up my father. I don't think they expect violence, but I bet they didn't expect it two weeks ago, either."

"Well, we've got the Feds on our side—I hope, anyway. Anyway, being in this home, I realize these people are no different than my people. I mean, they're nice as can be—feeding us, letting us sleep here, and treating us like we're family. If people would just realize..." Michael left the sentence unfinished.

Not knowing what to really expect, they fell asleep, feeling secure embraced in each other's arms.

Seven

Michael smelled coffee. He opened his eyes and was looking at Alan, whose eyes were closed. The rhythmic movement of his chest indicated he was still sleeping. Michael reached over and placed his hand gently on his chest, and he felt Alan's heartbeat through the white T-shirt he was wearing. "Alan," he whispered. "Hey, Alan, wake up."

He smelled bacon frying. "The others are up; they're fixing breakfast. I smell bacon."

Alan opened his eyes and smiled. "I love waking up next to you. Bacon or no bacon, I've got all the meat that I need right here," he said, and he kissed Michael and pulled him close.

"Quit, we can't do that here. Not now."

Michael pulled away and got out of bed. They got dressed and went to join the rest for breakfast. The blankets had all been put away and order returned to the house. George was reminded of the morning he saw Alan dropping Michael off for work and couldn't resist teasing them.

"I hope you two had a good night," he said, winking at Michael. Michael turned red and hoped the hosts weren't paying attention.

Breakfast consisted of bacon, ham, scrambled eggs, grits, biscuits, and gravy. Michael hadn't had a breakfast like that since leaving home, and he told them so.

"We need plenty of energy to start this journey," the woman replied, and they went over plans of how the march would begin, who would speak, and so forth.

They gathered around Brown Chapel, and there were more than three thousand people, mostly Negroes but a number of whites as well. Not all would complete the march, and others would join on the way. The air was chilly as they began, but spirits were high. Everyone was nervous as they walked the first few blocks to the bridge. No one knew if the Alabama national guardsmen, who were now under federal jurisdiction, were truly there to protect them or if they would ignore any threats or acts of violence. Michael and his friends were toward the back of the crowd as they turned onto U.S. 80, but soon they could see ahead as marchers climbed the rise of the bridge and continued walking without hesitation, and they felt a sense of relief.

The route was fifty-four miles long, and it took them through parts of Dallas, Lowndes, and Montgomery Counties. Many people wanted to take part in the march, but they knew they could not complete the entire distance, so they walked to the bridge and did not continue. Most of those planned to rejoin the march in Montgomery for the conclusion.

Michael took note of the armed military guards along the way. At some points, he would see an armed guard atop a hillside next to the road, and Michael couldn't decide if this made him feel safe or threatened. But after a few hours he was able to ignore the guards, and he spent time talking with other marchers and learning about their lives. He spoke with a pastor from Maine, a white man who had been involved in voter registration efforts across the Southeast. Two black men who had been arrested several times for attempting to register to vote told him what it felt like to be treated as second-class citizens. A man with only one leg, using crutches, was marching.

Some sang; some carried U.S. flags; some carried them upside down, signaling distress. Occasionally he would see people crying or hugging as they walked. Somewhere past a town called Casey they stopped to camp for the night at a farm owned by a man named David Hall. They slept under four huge tents, and the rest was much needed. Even though they had only walked about seven miles, the stress of the first couple of miles had added to their fatigue. The number of marchers had really decreased, to about three or four hundred, Michael estimated. He wondered if there would be any marchers left by the time they got to Montgomery. Some of those still in the group were his age or younger and seemed to have endless energy. Most, however, were already complaining of tired feet and blisters, but they vowed to continue.

The second day seemed long. Buses brought fresh marchers and picked up fatigued participants to take them back to Selma. The couple who had hosted the three left on the bus after explaining that the man could only take one day off from work, but they left the others assured that they would be in Montgomery for the final leg of the march and the speeches. Meanwhile, the new arrivals seemed to be full of energy, and they lifted the spirits of those who were tired.

For the most part the march was peaceful, but that was in spite of the overt racism that Michael was exposed to. There were protesters along the way, some with Confederate flags and some with signs such as "Who Needs Niggers," and "Niggers Out of Alabama." That was a word that Michael had heard in Tennessee but had never used himself. He had never heard Alan use it, but Michael asked him about it. Alan told him his father had used the word and that he had, too, as a kid, but once he began to rebel against his father he quit and would criticize his father for using it. "More out of a sense of making myself appear better than my father than from a sense that the word was wrong," he said. "Eventually I came to realize that the word was derogatory, but by that time I was already in the habit of using 'Negro' or 'black' instead."

They passed log shacks with tin roofs, with skinny dogs on the porches or cats underneath, and Michael noticed curious children watching, some holding onto their mothers' dresses, and others running toward the lines of marchers to get closer views. The adults would wave approvingly. Michael asked George why they weren't joining the march.

"These people are sharecroppers, and the land they live on belongs to white men. Most likely, they're afraid of repercussions if they're seen assisting us. It's sad, really, that they know they're being denied their rights, yet they're intimidated and can't even fight for what's theirs."

"It's unbelievable," Michael said. "They just seem so poor, yet they don't really seem unhappy—at least not as they watch us."

"They're a proud bunch of people, I'm sure. And their pride extends to us as they watch. I bet you didn't know this—of all the people in this county, Lowndes County, Alabama, of all the black people here, how many do you think are registered to vote?"

"I don't know, five percent, ten, maybe?"

"Not even close. There isn't a single registered black voter, even among those qualified, in Lowndes County. This is the most segregated place in Alabama. Worse than Selma. Worse than Birmingham, even."

Michael equated the sharecroppers' reluctance to participate out of fear of eviction by landlords to homosexuals having to hide their true identities out of fear of losing their jobs.

Michael also noticed that the countryside was much different than the farmland he was used to. They had reached a swampy area with Spanish moss hanging from the trees and fanlike palmettos on the ground. A marcher from Selma explained that the Spanish moss was still used by some to stuff mattresses, and the palmetto leaves were used for weaving baskets and hats. The local people had always "made do," she said, with what was at hand.

After walking for sixteen miles, they camped that night on land near a gas station called Rosie Steel's Grocery Store and Filling Station; it was owned by a seventy-eight-year-old widow. Michael was very aware of the National Guard MPs who were guarding the campsite, in part because the one who was stationed close by kept looking over at him and George, and not with contempt, it seemed, but with understanding. After a while Michael decided that the guardsman was probably homosexual, and he thought that his understanding may or may not have been about the protest at hand, but more likely was about his realization that his charges, at least these two, were like him. Michael shared his suspicion with Alan, who after a short glance replied, "No doubt. And a stud, too."

Michael was almost asleep when Alan whispered, "I'll be back in a jiff; I need to pee."

"OK," Michael replied without opening his eyes.

He was awakened by someone coughing, and he realized Alan had not returned. He didn't know how long he had been sleeping. He rose up on his elbows and looked around in the dim light and noticed that the MP was no longer at this post. A moment later he noticed the uniformed soldier approaching from a wooded area near the campsite. He returned to his designated post, looked around, and for a moment made eye contact with Michael, and then he quickly looked away.

A few minutes later, Michael saw Alan emerging from the same wooded area and realized the latrine area was in the opposite direction.

Michael closed his eyes and pretended to be asleep, in part because he didn't want to believe what was going through his mind, and partly because he knew he couldn't have the discussion with Alan that he wanted to in the middle of the night with all these people around.

The next morning Michael was quiet as he waited for an opportunity to confront Alan.

After they ate breakfast and before they began the day's journey, he pulled Alan aside and asked, "What did you and that national guardsman do last night? I saw you both come out of the woods, and that was nowhere near where you should have gone to pee."

"Nothing, Michael. I went over there because there was a line at the latrine, and I didn't want to wait. When I finished peeing, I turned and he was there, staring at me. I don't know what he was doing, and when he saw me looking at him, he turned around and left. That's it."

"Alan, I saw him come back, and he wouldn't even look me in the eye, and he had just about stared a hole in me earlier. He sure seemed guilty of something."

"Well, like I said, Michael, I don't know why he came over there, and I can't speak for him. Hell, why don't you ask the man? There he is, right over there," he responded angrily.

Alan was obviously upset at Michael's accusation, and he turned and walked away. Michael had no choice but to believe him, at least for the time being. He couldn't start an argument with Alan among the marchers. He thought about discussing it with George, the only other person in the group he really knew. *Where are you, George?* He had no one else to talk to about his suspicion. He caught up with Alan.

"I can't go ask him that. No telling what might happen if I accused a soldier of something like that. Just look at me. Tell me that nothing happened."

"Michael, I did not touch the man. Now, please, that's enough about that."

The group was preparing to leave, and George caught up with them and interrupted the conversation.

"Come on, you two, we're leaving."

Michael put aside his desire to talk to George about the situation with Alan because there was no privacy. He decided to accept Alan's terse explanation. For now at least.

The day's journey was routine—if one can consider the occasional racial slur and degrading sign routine. Michael was surprised at how his mind had adjusted—not to the point of accepting the hatred that he saw, but to where he wasn't shocked. They journeyed eleven miles that day, stopping for lunch and a short rest along the way. That night they camped on muddy land belonging to Robert Gardner. The rain and cold was getting to some of the marchers, but the knowledge that they were close to Montgomery gave them what they needed to continue.

~

On the fourth day, they passed a billboard with a picture of several men, both white and black, and an arrow pointing to one labeled as "King." The words at the top of the sign said "Martin Luther King at Communist Training Schools." George explained to Michael and Alan that others were trying to discredit King and convince the public to be suspicious of him because of the association that many civil rights leaders had with the Communist party in the past; the communists had been very supportive of civil rights when the Democratic and Republican parties were not, and Negro leaders had sought support from anyone they could find.

"Rustin was linked to communists, too," he said. "When Rustin was associated with the communists, they weren't known for the abuses we know of now. They were known for their promise of equality and freedom. He ended his association with them when he learned they were abandoning their support of equality and trading it for support of the USSR.

"But his biggest influence came from Gandhi. His principles of nonviolence are what Rustin is all about. And that is what our movement is all about now. He was beaten by police officers right outside of Nashville, near where we were the other day, for sitting at the front of a bus. He didn't fight back, and some of the white passengers were impressed, even to the point of complaining against the police at the station. He was released without charges pressed. Can you imagine what would have happened if he had fought back?"

As they approached Montgomery on March 24, their numbers swelled, and by the end of that day there were around four thousand marchers. Protesters increased in number as well, but Michael felt less threatened with the large numbers in their group. They camped that night at the Catholic St. Jude complex, within the city limits of Montgomery. They had made it, even though the next day would be more significant. That night, however, they relaxed and enjoyed entertainment by Peter, Paul, and Mary, Tony Bennett, Frankie Lane, and others.

Saturday morning, people kept arriving, causing disorganization, and they were late starting out for the final few miles of the walk. Protesters were out in numbers, as well, with signs such as "Run King Out of Alabama," and caricatures of a black man with "Will This Be Our New Uncle Sam?" on them. Michael saw a black man wearing a jacket with a stars-and-bars type flag and the words "Alabama God-Damn" painted on it. Whites were heckling the group and giving them the finger. A mixed group was carrying a sign that said, "Peace Corp Knows Integration Works." A group of nuns in black and white habits marched with them. Marchers near the front had large U.S. flags and a blue and white United Nations flag.

Eight

Eventually twenty-five thousand people were in front of the Alabama State Capitol to hear the dignitaries speak. Michael was swept up in the excitement and wondered how he could ever remember everything he was seeing and hearing to tell others. Who would he tell? He couldn't even answer *that* question.

While he waited, he studied the building in front of him. He was surprised at the similarity between the Alabama State Capitol and the U.S. Capitol, both white with a rounded dome and columns. Of course, the U.S. Capitol was larger. He thought it odd that the Alabama Capitol had a Confederate flag flying atop it, similar to many of the flags that the people protesting against the march carried.

He listened intently to the speakers, including his friend Bayard Rustin and then Dr. King. Dr. King's speech began as follows:

> My dear and abiding friends, Ralph Abernathy, and to all of the distinguished Americans seated here on the rostrum, my friends and coworkers of the state of Alabama, and to all of the freedom-loving people who have assembled here this afternoon from all over our nation and from all over the world: Last Sunday, more than eight thousand of us started on a mighty walk from Selma,

> Alabama. We have walked through desolate valleys and across the trying hills. We have walked on meandering highways and rested our bodies on rocky byways. Some of our faces are burned from the outpourings of the sweltering sun. Some have literally slept in the mud. We have been drenched by the rains. Our bodies are tired and our feet are somewhat sore.

Michael listened intently to Dr. King's speech, learning more about history, about Alabama's role in keeping the Negro down, about the struggle since reconstruction, the Bourbon privilege, and Jim Crow:

> If it may be said of the slavery era that the white man took the world and gave the Negro Jesus, then it may be said of the Reconstruction era that the southern aristocracy took the world and gave the poor white man Jim Crow. He gave him Jim Crow. And when his wrinkled stomach cried out for the food that his empty pockets could not provide, he ate Jim Crow, a psychological bird that told him that no matter how bad off he was, at least he was a white man, better than the black man. And he ate Jim Crow. And when his undernourished children cried out for the necessities that his low wages could not provide, he showed them the Jim Crow signs on the buses and in the stores, on the streets and in the public buildings. And his children, too, learned to feed upon Jim Crow, their last outpost of psychological oblivion.

Michael continued to listen closely, and his understanding of the power of the moment was underscored by Dr. King's words:

> Today I want to tell the city of Selma, today I want to say to the state of Alabama, today I want to say to the people of America and the nations of the world, that we are not about to turn around. We are on the move now.
>
> Yes, we are on the move and no wave of racism can stop us. We are on the move now.

Michael thought that rather than this just being *an* important event in history, that it might be the *most* important event in history—at least in the history he knew. This was the historical dividing line. Leaving the past was coming out of darkness, and entering the future was leading into brightness. A nation would become united. He forgot all about the protesters, the signs using the "N" word, the derogatory images, and the violence.

> Our aim must never be to defeat or humiliate the white man, but to win his friendship and understanding. We must come to see that the end we seek is a society at peace with itself, a society that can live with its conscience. And that will be a day not of the white man, not of the black man. That will be the day of man as man.

"That will be the day of man as man," Michael repeated to himself. Then to Alan he paraphrased, "A society at peace with itself that can live with its conscience will treat everyone fairly—the white man and the black man, the homosexual man and the heterosexual man. Man as man."

Michael moved closer to Alan, their bodies touching.

"All men, all people, should have equal treatment in society and under the law—how simple," he told his lover.

It was easy for Michael to equate racial equality to sexual equality in this crowd. It was all about equality, all about freedom. He looked around and noticed among the people a number of men whom he could imagine being homosexual, and he was reminded of the national guardsman and his issue with Alan but quickly put it out of his mind and returned his attention to what was happening in front of him. He understood why homosexuals would fight for the rights of blacks. The quest for—and the right of—equality was universal. It applied to everyone.

> How long? Not long, because the arc of the moral universe is long, but it bends toward justice.
>
> How long? Not long.

The speech ended amid thunderous applause and jubilation. The crowds began to disperse, and a group of dignitaries prepared to meet with the governor. A requirement was that all of those meeting had to be from Alabama, so Rustin was not among them. Michael was able to speak to him while he waited, and he offered congratulations. Then Michael asked Rustin a question.

"Mr. Rustin, I want to talk with you about your, uh, life. I, uh, we," he said, indicating Alan and himself, "are homosexuals. I understand that you are as well, and I, uh, want to discuss that."

"What would you want to know about me?" Rustin asked.

"No, not about you personally. About the way homosexuals are treated and what can be done about it."

"Oh. Well, I tell you what, son. I know that you work for one of the Tennessee senators. Gore? No, Bass—I remember. I'll look you up in Washington when I'm there, and we'll talk. I have been to places where homosexuality is not looked down on like it is here. Maybe there are changes in the future. The times, they are a-changing, as the song says."

"Thank you, sir. I look forward to talking with you."

∾

The three young men found their host couple, who had joined the crowd. They had brought George's car, as well as their own, so Michael and the rest wouldn't have to go back to Selma. Instead, they would spend the night in Montgomery and drive from there the next morning to Atlanta and on to DC that way. This was a fortunate decision because that evening a woman was murdered after taking marchers back to Selma. Viola Liuzzo had been assisted by a black man, Leroy Moton, and on her way to return him to Montgomery, their car had been chased by four white men who shot and killed her.

George, Alan, and Michael heard about this in the home they were staying in that night. Immediately the talk turned to "what ifs."

"What if we had been taking others back to Selma? We could have been the integrated car that was targeted," one of them said.

But just as quickly their conversation turned to Mrs. Liuzzo. They had all talked with her either in Selma or on the last day of the walk, and they had learned that she was a Unitarian Universalist Church member from Detroit who had been horrified at the events of March 7 in Selma and had decided on March 8 to go there. She was of the same denomination as Reverend Reeb, who had been beaten on March 9 and died on March 11.

They had met her at Brown Chapel where she was registering marchers, and on the night of March 24 she had joined the group at St. Jude. Michael had been able to talk with her that evening, and he had questioned her about the faith that she and Reeb had that pushed them to fight for the rights of others while people of other faiths, more common denominations in the South, seemed to be against equality, even to the point of embracing violence.

"She told me that she couldn't speak for what others believed, but that Abraham Lincoln had said that all men were created equal, that our Declaration of Independence said that all men were created equal, and that God himself created all men equal. She said she had grown up in the South—in Tennessee and Georgia, I believe she said—and had witnessed the hatred and inequality herself. She wasn't really some Yankee coming down here making trouble—she was returning to her homeland, trying to make things right. You know, I heard her telling one of the priests that she was anxious, that she thought somebody was going to be killed," Michael concluded.

They sat in silence for several minutes. Michael thought more about the conversation he'd had with Mrs. Liuzzo that night before she was murdered. After hearing Dr. King and now remembering what he had learned from Mrs. Liuzzo, he began to examine his own spiritual beliefs. He didn't know the actual tenets of the various denominations and sects, but he began to develop a belief that God would not put such hatred into man, so he would ignore any religion that promoted hatred. He also realized that God would not create any man in such a way as to make that man less equal than another, and that included race and sexuality, and so he would ignore any religion that exhibited such discrimination. Finally, he began to understand that love comes from God, all love, and if that love is between two men, or two women, for that matter, it is just as godly as if it were between a man and a woman, and so he would ignore any denomination that did not recognize this view of God's love. It was at this point that he had developed the ideals that would give him the direction he had set out to find less than three months before. But that didn't mean his life from here on out would be without conflict.

Because of Mrs. Liuzzo's murder, they decided that the next day they would return to Selma instead of going home. They thought they could learn more, and it seemed they should be able to pay some respects to her in some way there. For reasons of safety, Alan drove with Michael in the passenger seat and George lying down in the backseat. They did not want to be seen as an integrated car. Better to err on the side of caution, Alan had said, but when they passed the place where the murder had taken place, they slowed and all three looked out and were surprised at the number of state and federal agents around.

After making it safely back to Selma, the three men watched the news that evening. President Johnson spoke, calling the event "a tragedy and a stain on our American society." He personally announced the arrest of four men in the murder. He also vowed to exterminate the Ku Klux Klan. They learned that the four who were arrested were charged with "violating the civil rights of the murdered woman" and were members of the Bessemer Klavern of the

KKK. Michael remembered the suspicious looks they had received in Bessemer when they stopped there for gas.

Since they had returned to Selma, it made sense to return the same way they came, through north Alabama and Tennessee, but now the three felt anxious about driving through Bessemer. But they decided that with George lying down in back and covered with blankets and a suitcase to appear as if things were thrown in, they could breeze through and would make plans to get their gas somewhere else.

~

On Tuesday they began their trip back. They made a point to stop in Maplesville and tell Will about their experience. He had heard about the murder and about the march, but he had not seen any of the news on television because he didn't have one, and he couldn't get a signal where he lived even if he did. Michael had newspapers with pictures of the march, the speakers, and Mrs. Liuzzo, and he shared these with Will. Will couldn't read, but his granddaughter had seen the men get the newspapers out, and her curiosity had given her the courage to come out of the building. George got her to come over, and to their surprise, she was able to read most of the headlines and captions to the pictures to her grandfather. By the time they were ready to leave, Amylee Madison was sitting in Michael's lap, listening as George and Alan and he completed their story to her grandfather.

Michael sat her down and went to the car and opened the trunk.

"I've got something for you," he said. He had taken, with permission, several hand fans from Brown Chapel, and he gave her one. On it was a picture of Jesus reaching out to a little black girl about her size.

She thanked him and hugged him around his legs and said, "I love you."

Michael had to hold back tears and knelt down and hugged her back. “I love you, too. Now, you take good care of your grandpa, you hear me?”

“I will.”

Nine

They left Maplesville and decided they could make it past Bessemer and stop in College Hills, a section of Birmingham where they knew houses had been bombed, but they still felt better about that area than Bessemer, considering what they had seen on the television about Mrs. Liuzzo's killers. On the long drive from Birmingham to Nashville, Michael made an announcement.

"I want to stop in Franklin and see my parents."

"Are you crazy?" Alan asked. "I mean, what will you say?"

"I'm not sure. I just want them to know that I've taken part in this march and that I'm OK. Don't worry—I'm not going to tell them we're lovers or anything."

"That's not even my biggest worry," Alan said. "We've got a Negro with us, you know."

"Hey, I've got a name. I'm not just 'a Negro,'" George reminded them. "And I think I should get a say in this since my well-being could depend on it. Michael, what do you think your parents will do if you pull up with me in the car?"

"They will have to decide right then and there if they want me to remain their son," Michael said. "And I'm serious—with what I've learned on this trip about people and about God, they'll just have to see that. But I've not known them, either one, to be unreasonable and certainly not to be violent. I can't imagine anything happening."

Michael had not seen his family in three months, and he knew his mother and his little brother would be really upset if they found out he had been that close without coming by. George and Alan decided that they would only go along with it if he could somehow tell them that he was travelling with a black man before they got out of the car. Michael agreed and told them that he expected his father to be out working on the farm, and his mother would be home and his brother in school when they pulled up. They could drive the car around to the side of the house, away from the road, and he would go to the back door and tell his mother.

They pulled up after lunch but before school let out, and they drove around just as Michael had suggested. His mother was out back hanging laundry on the line, and she turned and saw the unfamiliar car pulling around. Michael got out and moved quickly away from the car in a direction that would keep her from seeing who was in it, and he called, "Mom!" and ran toward her.

"Michael!" she screamed and opened her arms as he reached her. "You're still growing, my goodness."

He spun around with her so that her back was to the car and immediately explained. "Mom, I've been on a trip, and I'm on the way back with some friends. One of them is a Negro. So is it OK if we stop here for a while and visit?"

She just stared at him and started crying.

"Mom, what's wrong?"

"Michael, we've been watching the news every night, and there's crazy stuff going on. That woman from up north getting killed in Alabama—you know she used to live in Tennessee."

"Mom, I know. Now, can they get out and come inside our house?" Michael was trying to remain calm.

She took a deep breath. "Yes, tell your friends to come over here."

Michael waved at the car for them to come, but they didn't get out. He walked over and told them to come on.

"George wouldn't let me get out. He wants to know what she said before he gets out on a white man's farm."

"She said OK, for ya'll to come on. So come on."

"What about your father?"

"We'll just have to wait, but if Mom says it's OK, he won't say a word."

"Wait, you mean she rules the roost? And you're the momma's boy, I guess," George joked.

"Shut up. Come on."

The three walked over to where Michael's mother was standing, and he introduced them. They could tell she had been crying, and they didn't know if it was from seeing her son for the first time in months or because of who he had with him. They didn't realize it was because of Viola Liuzzo's death. And what even Michael didn't know was that her death had affected his mom not just because she was a white woman who was killed, but because her death had put a damper on a glorious moment in history that she had been following.

"Your father has gone to the feed store and should be back in about half an hour. And your brother should be getting home soon, as well. They'll both be glad to see you. Ya'll come on in and get something to drink. And tell me where you've been. Michael says ya'll have been on a trip."

They all looked at each other with expectant expressions, waiting on someone else to speak.

Michael spoke. "Can we just wait until Daddy gets here and I can tell the story all at once? Besides, I want to know how you and Matthew and Dad are doing."

Matthew arrived home and ran into the house yelling, "Who's here?" He stopped when he saw the black man and the strange white man sitting at the table.

"These are my friends, Alan and George. This is my little brother, Matthew," Michael said, and then he walked over and popped Matthew on the shoulder. "Hey, little brother."

Matthew was going to be tall like his brother and was already almost six feet; he played basketball at school like Michael. George had noticed a goal out back on a dirt area and asked him if he wanted to shoot some baskets. He didn't want to be in the house when their father came home.

"Yeah, let me change clothes," Matthew said, and then he disappeared.

George got up and went outside to wait on Matthew.

Michael's father arrived home while Matthew and George were playing basketball. He stared for a moment at them and then went inside, thinking his wife would give a better explanation than his son would. In the house, he was surprised to see his older son and wondered who the other stranger was. Michael rose and walked over and reached out his hand, which his father took to give a slight acknowledgement. Michael introduced Alan and told his father that the man outside, George, was a friend of theirs.

"Who—what kind of friend—is George?"

Michael was not going to lie.

"He's a…" Michael hesitated and thought for a moment. "He's a civil rights worker. We're on our way back to DC from Selma and Montgomery."

Alan scooted his chair back in case he needed to make a quick exit.

"You mean you've been down there in that mess?" his father asked. "That's a bunch of troublemakers gettin' people killed is what it was. You're lucky to come back alive."

"Dad, we were safe; we knew what we were doing. George has been doing this a while, and he was even there that Sunday when so much happened a couple of weeks ago."

"Well, if you start bringing a bunch of Negroes around the house, people will start to talk. It might affect us selling our hay, even our cattle."

"That's ridiculous. First of all, I'm not gonna start bringing a bunch of people around the house. I don't know a bunch of Negroes, and I don't even live here now."

His dad was silent for a moment. "Well, maybe he can teach your brother to shoot free throws," was his response, in an effort to change the subject, and then he left the room.

Michael's mother jumped in. "Michael, that scares me to death, thinking you were down there."

Michael told her the story of Viola Liuzzo, that they had met and talked, and what he had learned from her. He didn't tell her the part about God's love extending to homosexuals—rather, he used inclusive terms such as "everyone" and "all people," which allowed her to assume he was referring to race. She listened with interest as he shared his revelations about religion and equality, unaware that equality between homosexuals and heterosexuals was as important in his understanding as equality among races.

"Listen," she said, "we were gonna surprise you, but we're gonna come to Washington and see you Easter weekend."

Michael and Alan looked at each other.

"What? What's wrong?" she asked.

"Nothing. Nothing at all." He thought quickly. "We, uh, I, uh, I thought for a minute we had another trip planned that, uh, week, but we don't. It's a different week."

"We thought we would come up and get a room where you're staying. Your brother can stay in your room. He's got spring break, and he'll be out of school."

Michael thought to himself that it was a good thing they had stopped and found this out as it would give them time to figure out what to do about their living arrangement. This made him anxious to leave, and he told them they had to get going but just wanted to stop and say hi.

"Dad, we're leaving," Michael hollered down the hallway that his dad had retreated to earlier.

He motioned for Alan to get up, and they all went outside, including Michael's father. Michael called George over and introduced him to his dad. George extended his hand. Michael's father hesitated and then took it and gave a weak handshake, something that Michael noticed.

His mother asked him to call the week before Easter and they would let him know what day they were coming and the other details. She asked Michael to take care of reserving the room for them, and he agreed.

In the car Michael repeated his thoughts out loud. "This is unbelievable. I had to stop and find this out? But I guess I'm glad. What if they had surprised us? At least this gives us time to figure out what to do."

"What *are* we going to do?" Alan asked. "You have to make a decision. If you go back to the motel and try to hide who you are, the clerk or somebody there will spill the beans that you moved out and then moved back in. If you stay where you are, with me, of course you'll have to tell them. Seems like those are your only two choices. I know what I think, but the decision is yours."

"I don't see any way out of it. What I have to do is figure out *how* to tell them. *What* to tell them. *When* to tell them."

"You two are in a fix," George said.

Not much more was said until they got to Nashville. Then it was all recounting their experiences in Alabama, and the future problem was forgotten about.

Ten

Back in Washington, Michael and Alan both were bombarded with questions about Alabama and the march and the murder. Michael returned to work on Thursday, and some of the questions to Michael from coworkers were rude and inappropriate. "What was it like travelling with a nigger?" a congressional aide from Georgia asked. "Did you have to sleep in their houses?"

The questions really annoyed Michael, and he either ignored them or corrected the assumptions that the "uneducated," as he called them, had. Other questions seemed worthy of answering. "Are the conditions of the Negroes in the South really as bad as reported? What kinds of people were protesting? You really knew and talked to that woman who was killed?" Those kinds of questions he didn't mind answering.

Both Senator Bass and Senator Gore spent time with Michael and also with Alan in order to learn more about the conditions in Alabama and progress on the voting issue. They were surprised to learn that in at least one county in Alabama there were no registered black voters.

But now there was another issue that consumed Michael's attention. His parents and brother would arrive in about three weeks. In the recesses of his mind, he knew that he would be telling his family the truth. And he should have been focusing on how he would tell them and when. But his mind wouldn't let him get past the "should I?" question.

This being Thursday, Alan and Michael's friends were expecting to see them at the bar to hear about their trip. Never mind it was their first day back at work, and they were still tired from the two-day ride in the '63 Olds. So they went, not expecting to stay late. While they were there, Frank appeared, Doc's friend whom Michael had met a few weeks earlier. Frank was hoping to find out more about their trip.

"I've been trying to keep up with the civil rights movement for a while. Not so much the details of specific events, but more of the process—how it's developing, how it's progressing."

"We met some people who could fill you in more than we could, probably," Michael told him. "What's your interest there?"

"I'm thinking—I've been thinking—that rights for homosexuals, the fight for rights, that is, could take the same path that civil rights is taking. I mean, we could follow them as a model—picketing, sit-ins, protests, you know. I think I told you we're already planning a protest here in the city."

"Yeah, you mentioned it. I want to hear more. But listen, we know a man, Bayard Rustin—have you heard of him? He's organized a lot of the civil rights events. He's going to be here soon, and he and I are planning to talk. Maybe he'll have some suggestions. Oh, he's homosexual, too."

"Never heard of him. Bring it up, then, if you can. And let me know. About our event, it's going to be in April. Some of us in the Society think it's a good idea to get going on this as soon as possible.

We've got to find ways to bring job inequality to the public's attention. I was fired for being homosexual. Others have been, too."

Michael was talking with Frank Kameny, the president of the Washington Mattachine Society, a group of homosexuals in DC that Michael remembered reading of in the *Post* articles. After Frank left, Doc explained that Frank and another man, Jack Nichols, formed the group in 1961, a few years after he was fired as an astronomer for the Army Map Service. Later that evening, Michael returned to the articles to help recall what he read, and he realized that Frank was the astronomer referred to in the series:

> Another of Washington's homosexuals is a former Government astronomer with a doctor's degree from Harvard...The astronomer speaks articulately of civil rights and job discrimination and cites studies in anthropology and psychoanalytic theory. Seven years ago he lost his Government job because of a report that he was a homosexual.
>
> "I decided that I had run long enough," he recalls. "All of us have to make our own compromises in life. I decided not to hide anymore."
>
> He fought his job dismissal in the courts. Since then he has appeared before a congressional subcommittee to speak for the local Mattachine Society and has defended homosexuality on radio and television programs.

Michael read on down: "He sometimes drops in at a 'gay' bar for conversation and a drink and attends the Mattachine meetings."

That was him. Michael was interested in the upcoming protests and told Alan that he hoped to talk with Frank more about it later. What he didn't know was that the first protest and his parents' visit would occur on the same day.

Michael had decided that there was no way to avoid telling his parents of his homosexuality. While in the city, they would discover that he and Alan were living together. He loved Alan, and that was becoming clear. He was not going to let anything come between them.

Bayard Rustin showed up at the congressional office the following week, and he and Michael went to lunch together. Rustin told him details about his life, including how and why he had acquired his accent, his affiliation with communism, and his adherence to the teachings of Gandhi. After about fifteen minutes of biography, Michael changed the subject. "What I want to know about is your sexuality. I mean, how did you know? And how did that affect you and your life, your career?"

"It would take more than a lunch hour to take you through all of that, Michael. But let me make you aware of a few things. I first became aware of my homosexual tendency while a student at Wilberforce, a college I attended in Ohio. I mentioned this to my grandmother, Julia Rustin, not giving her details, but letting her know that I preferred the company of guys. She knew what I meant. She asked if that was really what I enjoyed, and I told her I did. She said, 'Well, I suppose that's what you need to be.' She recognized that it was who I was, who I am, and she let it go at that. But because of the way she responded, I never felt the need to hide or pretend. Yes, be careful, as she advised, but hide, no."

"I'm dealing with some of that right now," Michael replied. "My parents are coming to visit in a couple of weeks. I'm living with my lover—you met him, Alan. What can we do but be honest?"

"That is the best way to handle it. Until you find out otherwise, you just have to have faith that your parents will be accepting of who you are and that their love will not depend on you being something that you're not."

"Well, that's a good way to look at it. I just need to figure out when to tell them—before they leave to come here or after they get here."

"I can't make that decision for you, Michael. You know them, and you know their particulars. If you want to guarantee that you see them, however, you should wait until they're here. Otherwise, they may not come. In addition, you will seem more of a man if you tell them in person."

"I guess you're right. I can't help thinking about Alan, though. His father...well, let's just say he had to find a new place to live and recover from an, altercation, let's call it."

"I was so fortunate to come from a family that was accepting," Rustin responded. "I think that seeing what discrimination and intolerance does to a society and to a family was part of that. Most white people don't know what that's about, so they don't consider it."

"Yeah, I see what you're talking about," Michael said.

Before the conversation ended, Michael recalled that he had told Frank he would try to get some information.

"Here's another thing. What about homosexuals who lose their jobs? A friend of mine is working on ideas to protest the firing of homosexuals for no other reason. What are your feelings on homosexual equality?" Michael asked.

"Michael, I think that all people should be treated with dignity and respect. And I believe that will come to pass one day. I do not know if that day will come soon, however.

"Let me tell you a story. I was a lot like you are now and about your age when I first began recognizing my homosexuality. Oh, I might have had a little inkling in high school, but athletics and studies took up most of my time, like with you. It was in college that I really became aware. But years later in California I got caught doing something I shouldn't have been doing. I might have even been set up, but anyway, I went to jail for about two months. Then I went into therapy. For many, many sessions a therapist tried to convince me that my homosexual desires were not valid. He never really convinced me of that, but he told me that the impulsive behavior that landed me in jail did not stem from my homosexual desires; rather, they came from my pride in myself. Self pride, to the point of putting my personal desires before those of the bigger cause for which I have fought and was fighting at the time. In other words, I should have been able to control those impulses and focus my energy on our cause.

"What I am trying to tell you is two things. One, don't let someone try to change what is in your mind by nature, and two, don't let the fact that you are homosexual keep you from whatever you decide your purpose should be.

"You should be able to be yourself, act responsibly, and have a happy and productive life. Those are not mutually exclusive."

"Well, I hope that I can do that," Michael responded.

Rustin continued as if Michael had not spoken. "I have travelled around the world, and among the places I have been is Norway, where I travelled with Dr. King when he went to accept his Nobel Peace Prize. In that country, homosexuals are not looked down upon. In fact, there is talk that this year or next their laws regarding homosexuals will be repealed. Most likely, they are the most advanced society in regard to homosexuality. But they have not spent years, decades really, fighting against the injustice of racism. In our country, there is deep hatred, and people, many of them, focus more on hatred and keeping us divided than on progress and unity. I would say advances here will be slow to come. The arc of the moral universe is long, but it bends toward justice. Those are Dr. King's words, remember?

"Mark my words, Michael. Once hatred of the blacks is overcome, then hatred of homosexuals will take its place."

He looked at Michael and nodded, letting him know it was now time to respond.

"Well, advances may be slow to come, but they won't be slow to begin. My friend Frank is talking of leading a protest later this month, here in this city. He has been following the civil rights movement and how it has progressed, and he wanted more information that he might be able to use. I'll tell him what you said, anyway."

"Tell him this: Two months ago I published an article where I explained that for our movement, the time of useful protests was drawing to a close. The protests and marches brought attention to our plight, but now it will require building coalitions and working in the political arenas. We have to build an effective political majority of our allies—the trade unions, liberals, religious groups. You saw this in Selma, groups coming together. And while certainly that was a big protest march, its purpose was to draw attention to the problem of voting rights. But those who were there, the Catholic nuns, the union members, they will go back and share their stories and their beliefs with others. And together, we can put pressure on the states and on Washington to make changes.

"As for homosexuals, you—we—will have to form those coalitions as well. We will have to start small. Christians, many of them, will be against you, just as they are against the Negro. And people don't understand homosexuality. They don't know homosexuals. We are invisible to most people. That is why being truthful with your parents is such an important step. And with others as well.

"What your friend is doing is admirable. Just as with that first sit-in at a diner or that first ride at the front of a bus, there is no predicting what the response will be. After this week, I won't be in Washington for a while, so I can't take part. But I wish you all well."

With that they finished up, and Rustin drove Michael back to work.

~

Michael decided to take Rustin's advice and wait until his family was in Washington to tell them. He learned later in the week that the protest was being planned for Saturday, April 17, Easter weekend, the weekend his parents would be there.

The plan was for Alan to accompany Michael when he told them. Realistic or not, they felt that with a witness present, tempers would be less likely to flare. Never mind that the witness would be the person who might be blamed for the bad news being delivered. Michael had made the reservations at the motel as requested, but their plan was to give directions to Alan's apartment and tell them there. Michael would tell them that he had moved when he talked to them before they left, but he would withhold the truth about why.

All seemed to go as planned until Michael made his phone call. It was Wednesday, the day before his parents were to leave, and when he called, his brother accepted the collect call.

"Hey, little man, let me talk to Mom."

"They're not here. They should be back any minute. I'm supposed to get the directions if you call, though."

They talked for a minute about Matthew's school and the end of basketball season, and then Michael started to give directions. "Got a pen? OK, first of all, I'm not living at the motel. I've moved to an apartment. Write this down."

"Wait, wait, wait. You've moved? Are you planning to stay in Washington? I mean, wouldn't you have to buy furniture and stuff?"

"Well, yeah. Listen, I'll tell y'all all about it when you get here. It just made more sense, and living in a motel was driving me crazy."

Michael gave him the directions to their apartment, and just as he was finishing up, Matthew said, "Hey, they just pulled up. Let me let you talk to Mom."

Michael could hear the receiver being set on the counter and Matthew telling his parents the news about him moving.

His mother got on the phone. "What's this I hear? You have an apartment?"

"Yes, Mother. Matthew has the directions."

He was afraid he would slip up, so he hurried to get off the phone. "This call has gone on too long; it's costing you."

~

The thought of telling his parents he was homosexual was making him anxious. Alan tried to reassure him, but how could words of comfort from a man whose father had beaten him and thrown him out of the house upon discovering his son was homosexual help? All Michael knew was that in less than forty-eight hours he would reveal his most private secret. Even though in most ways he now understood his sexuality to be natural and normal, at times he still felt some guilt and shame, and thus the apprehension. But there was no turning back now. The apartment had one bedroom, and it would be obvious when his family walked in that two people lived there. He thought that since they had met Alan the shock might be somewhat lessened. And what about Matthew? What would he think? Michael was supposed to be a role model for his little brother, and here he was about to shock him as well.

Michael took Friday afternoon off from work; everyone usually started their weekends early, anyway. After eating lunch he sat outside the apartment, waiting on the car from Tennessee to arrive. Alan was at work, but he had told Michael he would try to leave early, although Friday was often the busiest day of the week for grocery shopping.

Having nothing else to help him prepare, he brought the newspaper clippings out with him to read again, hoping to refresh his knowledge of the positive things they contained and to remind him of the things he might want to be on guard against. Along with the articles he had the folder that contained them so he could quickly slip them into hiding if necessary.

In the middle of the afternoon, a familiar two-tone Chevrolet Impala turned the corner, and Michael quickly put the folder away. The car parked on the opposite side of the street, and his family got out and stretched as Michael made his way across the street.

"So this is our capital," Matthew said.

"Just a few blocks that way is the Capitol and the White House and the things people come here to see," Michael replied.

As they crossed the street and entered the building, Michael began to explain.

"You need to know," he began hesitantly, "that I share the apartment with someone. With Alan, the man you met a couple of weeks ago."

Michael was getting anxious, and he refused to look anyone in the eye as they entered. He wanted to delay his news until Alan returned and quickly tried to change the subject.

"Anybody want something to drink? We have iced tea that we made or sodas. Oh, and the bathroom is right through there if anybody needs it."

None of the guests said a word as they entered and looked around. Matthew was the first to notice.

"Is that your room?" he asked. He followed quickly with, "Is there just one bedroom?"

Before either parent could comment, Michael answered, "One room, yes. Alan and I share it. "

His mother noticed that the room had just one bed and sat down on the couch to process the information. His father just stared at him.

Matthew spoke. "Well, me and you share a room at home, but we have two beds. I just see one bed in there."

Michael took a deep breath as if about to speak, but he couldn't.

His father asked, "Well, Michael, do you and your friend share that bed?"

Michael looked at his mother, who was clutching her purse for security and was beginning to cry.

"Mom, Dad, Matthew—yes, I share the bed with Alan. I'm, uh, I'm homosexual. And I love him. But that doesn't mean I'm any different from who you think I am." *Where is Alan?* Michael wondered. *He's supposed to be here for this.*

"Faggots and niggers? What next?" was his father's response.

"Dad, I've never heard you use that word," Michael responded, surprised.

"Well, it's just all these people. Different people. I'm not used to having black people in my home, and I'm not pleased to have someone acting like a faggot for a son. What's done this to you? This city? Your roommate? Damn, I don't know what to call him. Who's brought this on?"

"You can call him Alan—that's his name," Michael responded sarcastically. "Nobody brought anything on. I'm homosexual, and that's just the way it is. I guess I've been this way all along, but I just didn't realize it."

Everyone was silent for a moment.

"You know, this really doesn't surprise me. I guess the real shock is that you'd admit to it," his father charged.

Michael's mother finally spoke. "Michael, you need to pack up your things and come with us. We're taking you home."

"No, Mother," Michael tried to respond, but his father countered.

"He's not coming back to our house. I knew something was going on when he stopped by the house with that man. I didn't know what, but something. In fact, I've known something wasn't right with that boy for a long time," he continued, speaking as if Michael was not present.

Matthew jumped in, asking if he would have to share his room with a faggot, taking his cue from his father. Everyone seemed to be talking at once, and their voices began to get louder. Michael tried to quiet things down.

"Mom, Dad, stop. Matthew, shut up. Listen. Homosexuals, well, we're like anybody else. I've got friends here that…"

His dad interrupted. "I don't want to hear about any more of your sick friends. They're not friends of yours if they've got you acting like this."

"Dad, just listen. They are men who are educated. Astronomers. Some who work in the government. Alan runs a grocery store. There are doctors and medical workers. You wouldn't know anything was different about them. Psychologists and doctors…"

"Shrinks. Shit," his dad said, interrupting again.

"Psychologists and doctors," Michael said more slowly, "are learning that homosexuality is not a sickness. That a number of men just have a desire toward other men. It's the same with women."

"What would make you turn out this way?" his mother asked. "We tried to raise you right, as best we could."

She began to sob again.

Michael walked over and sat beside his mother. He put his arm around her and pulled her close.

His father had processed what Michael said earlier.

"Homos in our government? Running this country? No wonder Washington is so messed up."

"Dad, they're not running the country. But they work, like I work, for government people. Mom, I would never do anything to disappoint you on purpose. But this is just me. This is who I am."

"Does Ross know this?" his dad asked, thinking that it would be an embarrassment for his senator friend to find out.

"I don't know—I don't think so. But I know this. He's planning to take us all out to eat tonight. Somewhere nice. Including Alan. Now, you can make this into a scandal and embarrass the senator and the entire family, or we can all go and have a nice dinner with my boss.

"I know that this is a shock to you all. And it might take some getting used to—I don't know. But that's how it's going to be. You know, when I was first coming to terms with this, I thought everybody who saw me knew, like I had it stamped on my head or something. But they don't. So we can go out, have a good meal, and y'all can have time to think about this. But there is only one conclusion you can come to. Either you accept me like I am, or you don't. Either we remain a family, or we don't."

"Can you just take us to our motel or tell us how to get there?" his mom asked.

"Sure." As Michael answered, the door opened and Alan walked in.

"Y'all remember Alan."

It was obvious to Alan that things had not gone well, but he had decided what he would say regardless of the mood when he arrived home.

"Welcome to our nation's capital; hope your trip was OK."

No one responded. Alan just looked at them as Michael's parents and brother walked past him and out the door. Michael told Alan he would ride to the motel with them and walk back. It should take about thirty minutes, he said.

"Let me follow you all over there," Alan said. "I'll bring you back."

In the car everyone was silent. Michael and Matthew sat in the backseat. The motel was only a few blocks away, and as Michael gave directions for the final turn, his mother spoke to his father.

"This trip is ruined. Let's just turn around and start back home. Michael can come with us."

"No. I'm not going back home with you," Michael replied emphatically.

"Well then we can just drop you off, and we'll go home. You've got your ride back to your apartment, so," and then she directed her remarks to his father, "you can let him out here."

They were in front of the motel now, and they pulled into the parking lot. Matthew had remained silent since his initial response, but he was impressed by his big brother's resolve and the rebellion he perceived Michael was winning against his parents. He didn't really care if his brother was homosexual. Earlier he made the comment about sharing a room with a faggot just out of shock and as a way to enter the conversation. Now he just wanted to let his brother know he would accept him.

"I want to stay. This is my only chance to see Washington. And I don't want to go back and have to tell my friends we didn't see *anything* because my brother is a homo. Besides, he's still my brother."

Michael's father spoke up.

"Michael was right about one thing. We have an obligation to Ross, and it would be an embarrassment to him and to us for us to skip town without obliging his request to take us out to dinner. He has done our family a favor, and we can ignore this issue until after that dinner. But I do think that your friend should stay out of it."

"Alan?"

"Yeah, Alan. He's got no influence in this family. He's got nothing to do with our senator."

"Dad, sorry to burst your bubble. Alan has influence because he's family to me. And he does have something to do with our senator. After we returned from Alabama, both Bass and Gore met with us, and George, too, to find out about our trip and about the march. Senator Bass and Alan actually hit it off—I think more as a result of a preference for good bourbon than anything else. But Senator Bass is the one who asked that Alan come along. And I wouldn't be surprised if he knows—or suspects—that I'm homosexual. He knows Alan and I are living together, but we've never talked about it. I don't see why it should be brought up. Now, if Alan doesn't come, how are you going to explain that?"

His father responded, "You have just thrown this family into an awful mess. Now we have something we have to hide, and we're not used to having to keep secrets."

Michael's mother looked over at her husband and said, "Every family has secrets, so this is ours. But our family will survive this. We will go to dinner. And we will not mention this."

She turned toward the backseat.

"Matthew, that goes for you as well. Michael, continue with whatever you have to do to make dinner work. We'll deal with this later."

"It's all set up. Senator Bass is going to pick you three up here at seven thirty and then drive to our apartment and pick us up. Wear something nice, that's all I know."

~

The evening progressed without incident until near the end of dinner when Senator Bass asked what the family would be doing the next day. No one said anything for a few awkward moments. Eventually Michael spoke.

"They want to see the sights, and I think I can make a pretty good tour guide."

"Well, you all be careful tomorrow. There's a large protest planned against the war. Thousands of people are expected. We have these kinds of things all the time—no big deal for us—but you all aren't used to these kinds of crowds back home, and if you aren't used to it, they can be kind of scary," the senator warned.

Michael knew that the protest for job rights that Frank had organized would take place the next day also, but he kept that to himself.

At that time Michael and Senator Bass both noticed a familiar face coming toward them. The senator from out west whom Michael had gone home with had recognized both of them and was on his way over. Sitting at the table from which the senator arose was a young man, about Michael's age, watching the senator. Michael felt his stomach tighten up with several worries. Alan was not aware of Michael's history with the senator, Senator Bass didn't know they were acquainted, and his family would explode if they learned something had happened between them.

A sickening feeling came over Michael, and Alan noticed. Just as the senator got to the table, Alan silently mouthed, "What's wrong?"

"Ross, good to see you," the senator said as he extended his hand. "And Michael, isn't it? I hope things are getting better for you."

Michael felt himself blushing. Senator Bass introduced everyone around the table.

Alan noticed the young man at the senator's table, recognized him as being a hustler he knew from the bars, and he began to form an assumption. Why would the senator know Michael, and what did he mean about things getting better, he wondered. He would find out later.

The two senators commented to one another regarding some upcoming legislation, and then the western senator returned to his table.

~

Later that evening back in their apartment, Alan asked Michael how the senator knew him.

"I met him, uh, just in the office building," Michael responded unconvincingly.

"Really? Why would he say he hoped things were getting better? What does he know about you?"

"I don't know," Michael responded.

Alan could tell he was getting nervous, and he knew there was more to the story.

"Well, it seems that the man knows you, and you acted like a cat in a room full of rockers when he came over to the table, and he was there with a hustler I know from the bar. Now, what's going on?" he demanded.

"Nothing. Nothing has gone on. Come on, Alan."

"Come on, hell no. You're up there in that building with those senators every day, and the one who's palling around with a homo hustler wants to make sure you're OK. Now, what am I supposed to think?"

"Well, hell, Alan, what was I supposed to think when you and that hunky national guardsman emerged from the woods together in Alabama?"

Michael immediately realized that he didn't want to know any more about Alan and the guardsman. If he had, he would have brought it up earlier.

"Michael, I told you that I didn't touch the guy, and that's the truth. But I could have. Hell, if you've been whoring around with the senator, maybe I should have. To each his own."

"Alan," Michael started.

Alan, feeling sure that Michael was still seeing the senator, didn't let him continue.

"Yeah, the soldier boy followed me into the woods that night, but I didn't know it. I looked up from peeing, and there he was, just a few yards from me, with his dick in his hand, holding it, hard. Oh, and it was nice, too, Michael."

"Alan, please," Michael tried again.

"I walked a few steps closer so he could see mine, and it was getting hard, too. He started jerking off and took a step toward me, but I stepped back. I could have had it, Michael, but I didn't. I watched him get off, but I didn't. Oh, I was horny though, and I came back to get you to go back into the woods with me, but you were asleep, it seems.

"So I held back, Michael. I resisted. See, I decided that if I was going to be your lover, that I would change my ways and only have sex with you. Quite a change for me, Michael, and now I see that it might have been an unnecessary one."

Michael didn't know how to proceed. He had been holding a secret from his lover. Michael was not even sure what all had happened between him and the senator, but how could he explain spending the night over there and expect Alan to believe him? That had occurred before he and Alan were lovers, though, so it shouldn't be held against him any more than Alan's past should be held against him. And it was just one night, nothing more. He decided to tell him the story.

"Alan, here's what happened. Really, I'm not sure what did happen, but listen. Back in January, after we met—a week after you and I got together that first time—I was walking to the motel one night and met the senator. We got to talking, about the Senate and stuff. I went to his house, I got drunk, and I honestly don't remember what went on. As far as I'm concerned, nothing happened. He brought me back the next morning."

Alan believed that Michael was still seeing the senator.

"You fucked the senator, that's what happened. He's known for getting young guys to fuck him, and you've been used by the guy. Damn, Michael, how did you let yourself get...?"

He was unable to finish his sentence before Michael responded.

"Listen, I was so messed up back then, and he got me drunk. I wouldn't have done anything with him, I promise. I remember talking with him about us meeting in the park..."

"You what? He knows that I picked you up in the park? And what we did? And you were worried about me telling my friends about us?"

"He doesn't know it was *you*. I just told him it was a stranger. I didn't even know who you were at the time."

"Why would you even mention that to the senator? Oh wait, I get it. He was there tonight with a hustler. You were trying to hustle the guy?"

"No, I didn't go there for that. I don't even know what hustling is. Or I didn't until I learned from you about your life. Damn, Alan. I didn't go there hoping to have sex. But I just started drinking, and we got to talking, and it just came out about us, about what I had done. But listen, I don't know anything about him. I mean, I know he's married with kids about my age, but I don't understand what he's after. Or why. But he's the person who gave me the newspapers—those *Washington Post* papers that were about homosexuality."

"It just pisses me off that you've been seeing this guy. How many times? You were easy for me. I just walked up to you, and you let me suck you with no hesitation. Why should I think you weren't easy for him? I'm getting out of here." Alan was steamed.

"Wait, what do you mean? I didn't even know who you were then. And I don't even know what the senator and I did—if we really did anything at all. If I fucked him, I was too drunk to remember. And I only saw him that one time. So why are you leaving?"

"I've just got to think about this. Don't wait up."

Alan was out the door.

Michael was completely flustered. He had just let his parents know he was homosexual. He thought dinner had gone well, even though he knew his parents were faking their enjoyment. But then suddenly the man he loved walked out—with wrong assumptions and unwilling to believe the truth—right when he needed him there to talk to. He went to the bed and collapsed. He had anticipated lying here this night discussing with his lover his feelings about informing his parents and taking comfort from him. Instead, he was lying there alone, inexperienced at relationship issues, as he was with everything else about his life recently, not knowing what to do.

Again his thoughts returned to his only source of information about homosexuality, the words he had read in the newspapers. "One thing psychiatrists have discovered is that the homosexual is likely to be far more preoccupied and obsessed with the topic of sex than with most people."

Well, the conversation was all about sex, that's for sure, he thought.

He remembered how obsessed he had been after his first contact with Alan. He thought of Bayard Rustin's comments regarding impulsive behavior. Maybe he *had* gone to the senator's house looking for sex. Rustin was right—impulsive behavior leads to trouble.

Michael continued remembering lines from the articles. "The rules and practices of society tend to keep a man-woman marriage together even in the face of deep incompatibility. But society pressures tend to break up the homosexual couple. Without a community of interest centered on family and home, homosexual 'marriages' are not likely to survive the first disagreement."

Michael began to have his first doubts about his relationship with Alan since moving in with him. And with that, he began to wonder if being homosexual was where he wanted to be. He remembered Freud's letter: "If he is unhappy, neurotic, torn by conflicts, inhibited in his social life, analysis may bring him harmony, peace of mind, full efficiency, whether he remains a homosexual or gets changed."

Gets changed, he thought. He wondered if he needed to see a psychologist or a counselor of some kind. He decided that for now he would not consider that. To do so would be to admit something was wrong with him. It had taken weeks for him to convince himself that there was nothing wrong with being homosexual, and he wasn't about to retreat on that realization. What he didn't realize was that his parents were considering the very thing he was shielding his thoughts from: therapy.

His thoughts returned to Alan. When he met the senator and went to his house, he didn't even know Alan's name. Whatever he had done then, how could it be held against him now? He remembered what Mr. Rustin had told him about what his grandmother had said, that if that was what he enjoyed, then that was what he needed to do.

He recognized that he was being somewhat naïve in thinking his first relationship could be a lasting relationship, but at the same time, he asked himself, *Why not?*

"If I love this man—and I *do* love him—why can't it last?" he said out loud.

Michael fell asleep, alone for the first time in weeks, and he did not even wake up when Alan slipped into bed beside him.

Eleven

Alan was scheduled to work on Saturday, but he had planned to only go in for a couple of hours so that if things were working out, he could spend time with Michael and his family as they toured. Now he wasn't sure what to do. Michael woke up as Alan was getting ready to leave.

"I didn't even hear you come in. Are you about to leave?"

"Yeah, I told you I was going to work for a while today."

"So are you still coming home and going with us?"

"I don't know. Hell, I guess so. We need to talk, though. Not just about last night. We never decided what to do about Frank's protest. Those antiwar protesters will be out, too. Are we gonna get your folks involved in all of that?"

"I guess we'll just play it by ear. They're supposed to come here around ten o'clock, and we'll just walk over to the mall. We'll probably see the monument, the Lincoln and Jefferson memorials. If things are going OK, we can walk over to the White House where Frank's going to be."

"If things are going OK? What are the chances? This'll be a fun day!" Alan said sarcastically. "Gotta go."

"Don't be such a smart-ass," Michael countered. "And wait just a minute 'cause there's something I don't understand. You know, I needed you here last night. I know you don't have time to talk right now, but I can't figure out why my doing something with the senator when you and I weren't together is any different than what you told me you did to make money, fucking all those old men and all. And I'm not so sure about what happened in Alabama, either."

"I said I have to go," Alan replied angrily, and he slammed the door as he left.

He wasn't gone long, however, and he came back in while Michael was showering.

He called in to him. "Michael, I'm back. I couldn't get anything done at work—just told them I was leaving. When you get out, we'll talk. We've got a little while until they get here."

Alan returned to the living room and sat where he could see into the bedroom. He wanted to see Michael, hoping he would emerge from the bathroom like he often did, still drying himself off. Even though he was angry, he admired Michael's body and enjoyed seeing his partner naked.

Michael did as expected and noticed Alan staring.

"What are you looking at?" he asked, also angry.

"Michael, you are beautiful. You have the perfect body. I love every bit of you. But not just because of your body, and I've seen many. I love you because of your soul, your heart. I love you for what you've become. You are so tender, so caring, so smart. You are also so right.

"I shouldn't have gotten upset about whatever happened with you and the old senator. Maybe I was just a little jealous, thinking back to the old days—my old days. We should agree that whatever we did before we committed to each other is irrelevant. But I was thinking that being able to make important men happy, to have that bit of power over them, was mine, my deal, even though I don't do it anymore. It was a power that I had. Then you come along and get the big prize, a U.S. senator. But not that one because..."

"Hey, that's all nice, Alan," Michael interrupted. "Really, I appreciate it. But I have something bigger to worry about now."

"What's that?" Alan asked.

"Mom called from the motel. Last night after they dropped us off, Dad talked to Senator Bass about my *perversion*, as he called it. Senator Bass told them of a place I can go. No, a place they can *send* me to get cured. 'Changed' they called it. That's the same word I read in the paper. Mom said Bass had read about homosexuals being 'changed,' and I think he read the same newspaper articles I did. Anyway, he called them back this morning with the name of a place here that they want me to go to. A hospital. It was mentioned in the paper, too."

Michael had tears in his eyes.

"I don't want to be changed," he continued. "I don't want anything but you. They want to take this away from me. They want to ruin us."

Alan jumped up and ran to Michael, putting his arms around his naked body to comfort him.

"Michael, you don't have to do this. You're eighteen years old, almost nineteen. Your parents cannot take this away. I've known people who have gone to those places. They're like asylums. They shock you. They make you look at pictures of naked men, and if you start to get hard, they shock you again. They show you pictures of naked women and expect you to jerk off looking at them. That's supposed to make you heterosexual. Michael, they sometimes do things even worse."

Alan did not want to tell Michael that some homosexuals emerged from therapy in zombie-like states without any ability to function in society, yet they were considered cured.

Michael rested his head on Alan's shoulder as the tears began to run down his cheeks.

"What makes you think that? Mr. Rustin had therapy—he told me. He didn't mention anything like that. How do you know?" he asked between sobs.

"Michael, here is what I didn't finish telling you. This is what really had me upset about the senator. About a year ago, a kid from my hometown in Pennsylvania moved down here and looked me up. I knew of him, knew his family, but I didn't really know him. Anyway, he was running away from home; he was about sixteen or seventeen, but he looked even younger."

Alan led Michael over to the bed, and they sat down.

"His name was Juno—at least that's what everyone called him. He was homosexual, and his parents had found out, or were about to. He had been caught with another boy in school, in the restroom, and rather than face them, he ran away and came here. He stayed here; he slept on the couch, but we never did anything, I promise. He had been here about a week when somehow he met the senator, the same one who knows you.

"They were together in a park, in a fuckin' park," Alan said, beginning to get angry thinking about it. "They were caught, and somehow the fuckin' senator turns it all around, and Juno gets blamed. He refuses to tell them where he's from or what his name is, and he's hauled in. He gets committed to this place, and he's there for just a few days and goes through a bunch of this shit. Somehow he escapes—he told me he worked it out with an orderly to get out, so who knows what he really did. Anyway, he was such a cute, cute little kid. Looked like a cherub. But he was really messed up by then. Shows up here to get his stuff, and it's like he's on drugs or something. A few days later he's out in the evening. We were afraid to let him go anywhere by himself, but he was out alone that night, and these guys, one of them was an off-duty cop, the cop who had arrested him, he said, and two of his fag-hating buddies find him and beat the shit out of him. We wouldn't have ever known it except I came across him, just a couple of blocks from here, crumpled up in the gutter, bleeding. I thought he was dead.

"I shook him, and he cried out in pain. I was able to get him up and brought him back here. He rested a couple of days, and then one day when I came home…" Alan began to get choked up.

"One day, I came home and found him in the bathroom. Dead. Michael, he took his own life. He took a bunch of pills; I don't know where he got them."

Alan regained his composure, and his anger resurfaced.

"Michael, those fuckers—the senator, the doctors, the policeman and his asshole friends—they took his life. They don't give a shit about us, Michael. The doctors who do that, they're out to destroy us. Don't you dare let your parents send you to one of those places. That's why I got upset, Michael. That senator could have used his power to destroy you if it meant saving himself."

Michael was crying again.

"I don't know what to do, Alan," Michael said as he wiped his face. "They want to stay and check out that place on Monday. But they are so warped. They want to pretend everything is OK, to go sightseeing today and explore Washington. How fun! How can I spend time with them, knowing they want to put me away?"

"Michael, when you're homosexual, especially in this town, you have to learn to pretend," Alan suggested. "Pretend you're straight. Especially in government, where you work. Pretend you're amused when people are mocking us as queers or fags. You better learn to pretend things are OK even when they're not."

There was a knock at the door, and they realized Michael's family had arrived. Alan kissed Michael, and then he closed the door to the bedroom after telling him to get dressed and to do something about his eyes.

Michael's parents refused to come into the apartment, but Matthew spoke up.

"I'm not ashamed of my brother."

Apparently he knows what the parents are doing and doesn't like it, Alan thought.

Matthew pushed his way in, muttering, "They're the crazy ones."

Alan followed him in, half closing the door. "What's going on? Yesterday you were calling your brother a fag and seemed to not care about him. Now what?"

"I heard my parents talking last night. I don't really know what to think of Michael being a homosexual, but I don't like hearing our parents talk that way about him. They talked like he wasn't even part of the family, like he was some kind of sick and crazy freak. He's not—he's my brother."

"Well, he's certainly not happy about what your parents want to do."

"They don't even know what they're getting him into. They talked with Mr. Bass and got the name of a hospital. I think they want to put him in a crazy place or something. They can't do this to him."

Matthew was getting emotional, and Alan knew Michael would appear from the bedroom soon.

"Well, come on, straighten up. Your brother is upset enough; he doesn't need to see you getting messed up."

Michael came into the room and said glumly, "Hey, Matt, where's Mom and Dad?"

"Outside waiting. Damn, you look like shit."

"I can't help it. I, uh, got shampoo in my eyes. Come on, let's go."

Twelve

April 17, 1965, was an important day as far as protests go. Civil rights workers, fresh off the successful march in Alabama, were set to protest a government that would ignore, it seemed, the plight of its own citizens in the South, but would enter a war on the other side of the world. College students were restless and concerned about the quality of education they were getting. Homosexuals were beginning to realize that their sexual preference was normal, that they were not the sick people they had been made out to be.

Michael took Alan's advice and tried to act as if nothing was going on. They walked, with Michael's family, toward the mall, unaware of the size of the antiwar protest that was being assembled at the time. Michael had seen on the news that up to two thousand protesters were expected, but as they made their way past the Capitol, they saw what must have been fifteen or twenty thousand people gathering close to the Washington Monument. The first large protest against the Vietnam War, organized by the Students for a Democratic Society, was taking place, and it compared in size to the crowd that Michael and Alan had been a part of in Montgomery.

Michael at first planned to lead his family around the crowd, to make their way to the Lincoln Memorial, but as they got closer, he noticed that a number of protesters were Negroes, and he recognized some from the Alabama trip. As he scanned the crowd, he saw George and Isaiah, so he made his way to them.

"George! Isaiah! Hey!" he called. "You remember all these people, my mom and my dad and brother. Oh, this is Isaiah," he said to his family, remembering that Isaiah had not been with them when they stopped at the farm. "Isaiah, this is my mother and father and my little brother, Matthew."

"Big crowd for this protest, huh?" George said.

"Yeah, I had no idea from the paper that it would be this big," Michael replied.

"I don't think they were considering that the black people would join in, but the truth is, we don't like our government spending money over there fighting somebody else's war when we still have poverty here and we know that black folks still can't vote in Alabama."

"Well, that makes sense."

Just seeing the crowd, being reminded of how he had felt in the crowd in Montgomery, and then running into George here gave Michael confidence. He decided to take his family on to the Lincoln Memorial as planned and then to the White House, where the protest that Frank had organized would take place.

"This is too crowded. We can come back later to see the monument," he told his family. "Let's go see the Lincoln Memorial."

The Lincoln Memorial had a crowd around it, too, including protesters as well as everyday tourists. Michael had been to the base of the memorial, but he had never been up the stairs, so he led his family up to see the statue of the former president up close. They were surprised at how big the statue was, and although their parents did not seem interested, Michael and Matthew took time to read the Gettysburg Address, which was inscribed on one of the walls. The words "All men are created equal" and "that this nation, under God, shall have a new birth of freedom" stayed with Michael, and a sense of pride began to grow. In view of what he had learned this morning, a new birth of freedom to him would be a break from his parents.

They then read Lincoln's second inaugural address, which was inscribed on another wall. From it the phrase "let us strive on to finish the work we are in" reminded him of Bayard Rustin's words regarding the importance of priorities and working for the bigger cause, whatever that might be, and his pride turned to courage. He hoped that when he got to the White House, the protesters would still be there.

He led his family back through the crowd and stopped to listen to the speaker. He knew this would irritate his parents, and that didn't bother him. He just wanted to take a few minutes to plan what he would say when they got to the homosexual picket. Soon, however, the antiwar crowd began to close in on them, and he led his family away from there and toward the White House.

The White House was not far from the mall, and they were there in just a few minutes. They came across ten or so protesters carrying hand-lettered signs supporting equality for homosexuals, with such messages as "Fifteen Million U.S. Homosexuals Protest Federal Treatment" and "Discrimination Against Homosexuals Is as Immoral as Discrimination Against Negroes and Jews." Others read "Private Consenting Sexual Conduct by Adults Is NOT the Government's Concern" and "Homosexual Citizens Want Equality of Job Opportunity."

Michael walked right up to the protesters and said, "This is my family. They learned on their trip to Washington that I'm a homosexual. Now they want to put me away. Please help me show them that homosexuals are normal people, that we're just like everyone else."

No mention had been made by his parents of their decision to insist on treatment for Michael, and he thought this would be a good time to bring it up. For him, this was a way of publicly acknowledging his homosexuality in front of his parents since most of the people in the protest already knew. He was not trying to embarrass his mother or father; he was letting them know that he was not ashamed of his sexuality and that by seeing normal, well-dressed men and women who were homosexual that his parents would see that he could be this way and still live a normal life. He also hoped that Frank and the others were knowledgeable about the therapy issue and that they would help put a stop to what his parents wanted to do.

His mother tried to interrupt, but Michael continued. "They act like I'm not even human, like I'm some sort of sick animal."

When he made this statement, he almost choked up as he realized what his parents really thought of him. He was close to tears, and he decided not to go on, not wanting to lose control in front of the marchers. Alan could tell Michael needed support, so he stepped over close to him, as did Matthew. Frank left the protest line and joined them.

One of the protesters, a woman, leaned her sign against the fence and walked over to Michael's mother and father and talked with them about tales she had heard about young homosexuals being sent to therapy for change. She told them that the latest research in the medical and psychology fields showed that being homosexual was not a sickness and not a choice, and not something that could or should be treated. She also told them some of the gruesome details of therapy, describing it as inhumane. Michael's mother began to cry, and the protester put her arms around her.

"What do we do?" Michael's mother asked.

"You love your son, that's what you do. I have a child myself. Loving him is the easiest thing in the world for me. But sometimes it can be the hardest thing in the world. Yet still, that boy is a part of me, and I will love him regardless of what he does."

Michael's father, true to form, stayed out of the conversation. He rarely made conversation with his friends, and he certainly wasn't going to do so with these strangers who had nothing to do with his life.

Instead, he stood in silence and read as protesters passed by with more signs: "Sexual preference is irrelevant to federal employment" and "Equal opportunity for all...all means ALL!"

The protesters were familiar with the drama that was unfolding before them. They had all been rejected in one way or another because of their sexuality, though some had eventually been accepted by their families.

One thing was certain: sightseeing for the day was over.

Alan said, "I, uh, we, are going back to my apartment. We might stop and get something to eat. You're welcome to come with us, but you are *not* welcome if you think you're going to take him away from me."

With that, Alan and Michael began walking. A moment later, the others followed. Alan put his arm around Michael's shoulder, not so much in the way a lover might, but more as a supportive measure.

"We'll get through this," he told his lover, "and I meant that about not letting them take you away."

In spite of the courage that Michael exhibited at the rally, he now felt defeated. What was his mother thinking? His father? Would they accept his decision to live as he believed he was created to live? Was he about to lose his family for real?

Alan and Michael went into the café where they had talked before. They watched as Michael's family walked by without his parents looking in. Matthew looked in and shrugged his shoulders.

A few seconds later Matthew came back and entered the café and sat next to Michael, telling him, "I don't know what they're doing.

Neither one will say a thing. I love you, though, Michael. And if you're happy with Alan, then I say do what makes you happy."

"Why this change of heart? Yesterday you acted like you couldn't care less about me. I mean, I appreciate the support, but what gives?"

"When you told us yesterday that you were a homosexual," he began in a half whisper, "it hit me like a ton of bricks. But listening to them last night, talking about you as if you're less than human, made me feel uncomfortable. Dad used the same tone he used after your visit last month, after you brought that black man into the house."

"What are you talking about? What tone?"

"After you left, he said he didn't appreciate you bringing him into the house, and he used a word we don't like to use. Mom was all for the advances we were hearing about on the news, and I thought Dad was just ignoring it, like he always does. But that day I realized how hateful he is."

Matthew's voice turned to a whisper, "Toward Negroes. They got in a huge argument. So yesterday when I saw him being so hateful toward you, it just made me think that this hatred, maybe it's just as unfounded as his hatred toward black people. Michael, it's been awful living with them this last month."

"Matt, I wish we had time to talk more, me and you. There's so much that you don't know—at least, I don't know how you could know—about race and the civil rights movement. Mom is on the right side of this, the right side of history. Dad will be left behind if he doesn't change.

"But they're both on the wrong side of the issue I'm dealing with. I have learned from listening to people, people much more experienced and smarter than me, that equality is not something to be dished out on a selective basis, and that equality begins with respect.

"But I also learned that sometimes you have to give up something to fight for a bigger cause. And if I have to give them up, I will. I hope and I pray that they'll come around. But I already live away from home; I rarely see them. I can do without them if I have to."

"Well, listen, I'll try to keep you informed about what's going on. But I need to go, to catch up with them. I'll talk to you tonight."

"OK, Matt. Take care."

He gave his brother a hug, and then he left to join his parents.

When Michael didn't hear from them that evening regarding dinner, he talked Alan into driving him over to the motel. They didn't see the family car in front of the room, and Michael thought they might have gone to dinner without him. But when he checked with the desk clerk, he learned that they had checked out earlier in the afternoon.

"Oh, they said to give you this," the clerk said as he handed Michael an envelope.

Back at the apartment, Michael lay on the bed clutching the envelope. He was hesitant to open it, afraid of what he might read.

"How long are you going to wait before you open that?" Alan asked. "Whatever it says, it's not going to change, so you might as well read it."

Michael sat up. "It might just be better if I don't know. Maybe I should just throw it away. I could burn it."

"Michael, even if you do that, whatever feelings are expressed in that envelope will still live. Ignoring them won't change the way your family feels about you. And whatever it says isn't going to change the way I feel about you. But by not opening it, you're just tormenting yourself."

Michael asked for a glass of scotch and drank it while he tapped the envelope on the nightstand. He used his fingernails and slowly tore the end of the envelope, and then he blew into it to open it. He peered inside. A single sheet of folded paper was inside. He pulled it out and recognized his mother's handwriting. He began to read aloud.

"My dearest Michael, I don't understand what has caused you to do this. I only know that the Michael I just saw is not the Michael I know. For eighteen years we have raised you, raised you as best we could, we thought. But I always knew something was not right. When your brother came along there was a difference that only I as a mother might notice. But as you aged, I could tell that something about you, a nurturing type of spirit, made you different. Remember your calf?"

Michael recalled a newborn calf that was sickly when he was about eight years old. His father had wanted to put the calf down, but Michael cried and wouldn't let it happen. He took the calf up to the house and nursed it back to health, even as his parents protested that he was wasting his time. The calf later became one of their best producers.

"She died on the day you called back in February. I could tell something wasn't right when you called. I thought somehow you knew about the cow. Now I know it wasn't about that at all."

Michael's eyes were filling with tears as he turned the paper over.

"When I put you on that bus to come here, I had a thought that I might never see you again. As the bus pulled away, I cried. *There goes my baby*, I thought, *to an unknown place. What will he discover?* I never expected this."

Michael thought back to the day he got off the bus and what all had happened in his first few weeks in Washington. He remembered the fear he had felt in the senator's kitchen after waking up in his home, a situation he had never expected as well. He continued to read. "When you pulled up last month with your friends, I didn't know what to think. I didn't know whether to be proud or frightened. As you left that day, pride won out. You were doing the right thing. Your father didn't think so, but I did. But now you have taken things too far. Your father is blaming me for this. Your brother is upset at both of us. Our family is torn. Please, Michael, think of what you are doing to our family. Think of what you are doing to me, to your brother, to your father. One of the women who was protesting hugged me and told me to love my son. I am trying, Michael. I am trying."

Michael looked at Alan. She had only signed it "Your mother." No "love, Mother" or "I love you."

Alan moved over to the bed and put his arm around his lover. Michael rested his head on Alan's shoulder.

"I'm your family now, Michael. In time, your parents may come around, but for now and for the future, I am your family."

Michael tried to put it all together, but his mind wasn't ready to accept losing his family. He remembered the words of Bayard Rustin speaking of his grandmother's acceptance: "She recognized that it was who I was, who I am, and let it go at that."

He realized that it wasn't asking too much to expect acceptance from his family.

He recalled his conversation with Viola Liuzzo and his understanding from her that all men are created equal in the eyes of God and in the eyes of our founding fathers. He realized that it wasn't asking too much to expect equality from his government.

He remembered the day in Montgomery and Martin Luther King saying "the day of man and man," and his feeling at that moment that not just the white man and the black man, but the homosexual man and the heterosexual man could be part of that day. He realized that it wasn't asking too much to be accepted by society.

He suddenly remembered Will, the man from Maplesville, who had quoted Abraham Lincoln: "Whatever you are, be a good one." He thought of the Negro couple in Selma that had treated Alan and him like family. He realized that it wasn't asking too much to be accepted by his own family.

He went to the dresser and pulled a small box out of his drawer. From it, he removed a folded piece of paper which contained a penny, the one that Will had given him. "Where's yours?" he asked Alan.

Alan retrieved his penny, and Michael took them both and held them together with the Lincoln faces together. He pulled Alan close.

"When we were in Tennessee with George, I was prepared to give up my family if they wouldn't support the rights of the Negro. Remember? Those weren't just empty words, Alan. If they hadn't allowed George to come inside, I would have left. If I'll stand in support of him and in support of his race, there is no reason for me not to stand in support of myself. And of you. In time, I hope they will understand, but until they do, I can only do one thing."

The sense of freedom that Michael had felt in the Lincoln Memorial returned. Even with the loss of his family, he felt a heavy burden had been lifted from his shoulders. And he knew that the man sitting next to him was the person he wanted to spend his life with.

"I will be the best man—the best partner to you—that I can be. We'll be a family, and we'll be a good one. These two pennies, together in this box, will represent our bond."

"Michael, I would be honored to share my life with you. You are a blessing to me, and I have learned so much since knowing you. You have helped me to become a better person, and I love you. I really do love you."

"I love you, too, Alan."

With that, they kissed. A long, passionate, meaningful kiss. Then they left to go celebrate the protest with Frank and those others.

Epilogue

It would be a year before Michael saw his parents again. Matt was about to finish high school and had sent an invitation, addressed to "Michael and Alan" with no last names. But it was the first piece of mail that Michael had received from home that included both their names in any form.

He had received a birthday card and two brief notes from his mother about his father's health, which had begun to fail during the heat of the summer, but those were addressed only to him.

"You should go," said Alan. "I've watched you each time a letter came from home. I can tell that you still have feelings for your parents. Besides, you have a lot to tell them."

After Senator Bass had recommended therapy to his parents, Michael had not felt comfortable working for him. He had asked Senator Gore if he could work in his office, and Senator Bass agreed to the change.

On August 4, 1965, Michael was sitting in the gallery when both Senators Bass and Gore voted in favor of the Voting Rights Act. Two days later, Alan and George accompanied him as he watched President Johnson sign the bill into law. On that day, he confided in Senator Gore that he wanted to become a lawyer, and the senator helped him get into college. On his college application he wrote that he wanted to work for civil rights for all people.

In his first semester he made all As and was about to do the same the second semester and be named to the dean's list.

Alan was right. Michael did have news to share, and he decided to go. "But only if you go with me," he said. "After all, the invitation is addressed to both of us."

It didn't take much convincing before Alan agreed to go for two reasons. He didn't trust Michael's parents and was afraid he might not see his lover again if he didn't go. But most of all, he wanted to be there when they learned how successful their son was becoming in college. Alan was proud of his partner.

They went to Tennessee and attended the graduation, where they saw Michael's parents for the first time since their trip to Washington. His parents didn't have much to say, but Michael and Matthew had a lot of catching up to do. Michael could tell that his mother was listening, and though she didn't respond, he could tell by her expressions that she was proud of his accomplishments.

The next morning a sliver of sunlight crossed Michael's face as he lay in the strange motel bed, and he opened his eyes. He thought about the previous evening. According to the articles he had read, he wasn't supposed to be happy, but he had an indication that he had just regained his family. He felt the arms wrapped around him, and it was not his imagination this time. *Could this be happening? Could I have both my family and my lover?* He pondered these things as he snuggled closer to Alan's warmth. Michael smiled as he fell back asleep.

The Articles

The following articles were printed in the *Washington Post* in 1965. They were collected and given to my uncle, Dr. Joseph Openshaw, who resided in Washington, DC, at the time, by Richard Devan. My uncle mailed the original articles, cut from the paper, to me in 2008, and they became the basis for this book. They are reproduced here in unaltered form, as printed in 1965.

The Washington Post

Sunday, Jan. 31, 1965

Those Others: A Report on Homosexuality

First of a Series

By Jean M. White

Washington Post Staff Writer

This series of articles would not have been written five years ago.

Then, a frank and open discussion of homosexuality would have been impossible. It was a topic not to be mentioned in polite society or public print because it could be distasteful, embarrassing and disturbing.

So, like mental illness and venereal disease earlier, homosexuality was stored out of sight in society's attic, carefully hidden under a blanket of silence—except for snide jokes or oblique allusions.

Now, there is a growing awareness and concern about the problem of homosexuality—brought about in part by a more open and liberal public attitude toward sex in general.

In recent years, the subject has been debated in the British parliament, discussed in statements by doctors, lawyers and churchmen and examined, if somewhat gingerly, in the public media.

The conspiracy of silence of the past nurtured myths, misconceptions, false stereotypes and feelings of disgust and revulsion. They still cloud any discussion of homosexuality. But more and more, recognition has come of a need to reappraise our laws—and our attitudes.

The Troubling Questions

Society-at-large faces a practical problem. It must decide how it is going to deal with the homosexual in its midst. And this decision, in turn, raises a troubling complexity of legal, medical, moral, and religious questions.

Now, for the first time, some of these questions are being asked in public:

- Are homosexuals born or made by environment? Is homosexuality a crime, disease, choice or natural way of life for a minority?
- Are there more homosexuals today than heretofore and do they pose a threat to the structure and moral fiber of society?
- Can homosexuality be treated, and if it can, should it be?
- With all society's hostility, is the homosexual life really "gay"? Are there any happy, well-adjusted, socially productive homosexuals?
- Are present laws unnecessarily harsh and punitive toward homosexuals? Should law reach into the bedroom in the area of private morals? Can laws be revised to assure compassionate and fair treatment of homosexuals and still protect public decency and children?
- Should homosexuals be fired automatically from government jobs, sensitive or nonsensitive? Should they be cashiered out of the armed forces with the stigma of "less-than-honorable" discharges?
- Is homosexuality here to stay? Can it be prevented?

Focus on the Male

Because of the growing need for answers to these questions, medical and legal spokesmen have been calling for more open discussion to ventilate this social problem.

This series of articles will deal mainly with the male homosexual because female homosexuality poses less of a social problem.

The Lesbian has been treated more tolerantly by society and seldom comes into conflict with the law, perhaps because she generally is less aggressive in her sexual pursuits and because our culture allows a more open display of affection between women.

By medical definition, the term "homosexual" should be used only when sexual activity with the same sex is repeatedly or exclusively preferred after adolescence.

Homosexuality and heterosexuality are not necessarily mutually exclusive. Some homosexuals lead "double lives." They marry and have children. There may be intervals of months, even years, between homosexual contacts. But there still is a repetitive pattern of behavior.

One isolated homosexual experience doesn't make a "homosexual" just as one drink doesn't make an alcoholic. Boys often experiment behind the barn as a common phase of sexual development. In an atmosphere of high spirits and low inhibitions at a stag party, an incident may occur, never to be repeated.

Whether or not there are more homosexuals today than there once were, they certainly are more visible.

In the larger cities, avowed homosexuals have congregated in "gay" colonies. They walk along the streets in tight-cut pants, with long hair and short jackets, and unabashedly declare their homosexuality for the world to see. They have their own bars, haberdashers, "cruising" grounds, bikinis, swimming beaches and even a kind of lavender Baedeker called the "Gay Guide to Europe."

These exhibitionist streetwalkers have high visibility but are only one small fringe.

Another visible group centers around the organized homophile organizations, which attract an entirely different type of avowed, militant homosexual.

These are the intellectual clubs with such playful names as One, Inc.; Janus Society (after the Roman god with opposite faces); Daughters of Bilitis (a poet of fiction who was modeled after Sappho of Lesbos), and the Mattachine Society (named for medieval court jesters permitted to utter painful truths from behind their masks).

Members of these clubs worry about public relations and the "image" of the homosexual.

They publish magazines, hold meetings to hear doctors and clergymen, hire lawyers to fight job dismissals and ask for social equality for what they like to call the "Nation's second largest minority."

These "organization" homosexuals disown the "flaming faggots" who swish along the street and the compulsive and potentially violent perverts who haunt public restrooms and parks.

Furtive and Lonely

Most homosexuals, however, try to pass in the "straight" heterosexual world. And most live out their lives without a brush with the law or an attention-attracting incident. Some observers have estimated that perhaps 85 per cent go undetected.

In large cities, some middle-class homosexuals with good jobs have fashioned a sub-culture in which they can live quite pleasantly. They have a social and personal life insulated from society's disapproval. At in-group cocktail parties, dinners and week end beach gatherings, they can drop the mask worn in everyday living.

But for most of the hidden homosexuals, it is a furtive, lonely life of passing attachments, a life haunted by fear of exposure, loss of job, blackmail and perhaps guilt. It is gay only in homosexual jargon.

There are as many layers to the homosexual community as exist in heterosexual society. Homosexuality cuts across all ages, professions, trades, city–small town–rural backgrounds and social, educational and personality groups.

'Hollywood House' Set

Take 25-year-old David, who belongs to the "Hollywood House" set in Washington.

A big event on the set's social calendar is the "high-drag" dance on Halloween or special occasions like the gala inauguration of the group's own president and "first lady." Then, under the camouflage of a masquerade ball, the members can dress in women's clothes and dance together. (This behavior, another homosexual outside the Hollywood set wanted to explain, is prompted not so much by a desire to wear women's attire as the wish to "thumb the nose" at society and caricature the public's stereotype of a homosexual.)

Yet members of the Hollywood House set live an existence that is part masquerade itself.

David and his friends adopt pseudonyms: his is Perry Mason; a friend is Liz Taylor. They use these pseudonyms to gossip about current couples and romantic affairs within the group. Each year they hold an "Academy Award" dinner to honor the best actor and actress in the set.

David agrees that homosexuals should not affront public decency with acts in public restrooms and parks. Yet he says he was once arrested at Hains Point.

How does he explain this?

"I looked around and saw stray heterosexuals were making out all around me. So why shouldn't I? Why pick on us?"

Then, he adds: "We're headed for another Sodom and Gomorrah. But I can't stop."

David says that he once went to St. Elizabeths to try to change but "it didn't take" even though he has a background of heterosexual reactions.

Another of Washington's homosexuals is a former Government astronomer with a doctor's degree from Harvard. He and David seem to have in common only a preference for male sex partners.

The astronomer speaks articulately of civil rights and job discrimination and cites studies in anthropology and psychoanalytic theory. Seven years ago he lost his Government job because of a report that he was a homosexual.

"I decided then that I had run long enough," he recalls. "All of us have to make our own compromises in life. I decided not to hide anymore."

He fought his job dismissal in the courts. Since then he has appeared before a congressional subcommittee to speak for the local Mattachine Society and has defended homosexuality on radio and television programs.

After long months without work and then a temporary job as a technician, he finally was hired as a physicist a year ago by a private employer, who knows he is a homosexual.

This middle-class homosexual with college degrees deplores the perverts and "queens" and points out that heterosexuals also have their rapists, child molesters, sadists and neurotics. He sometimes drops in at a "gay" bar for conversation and a drink and attends the Mattachine meetings. He has sought a lasting relationship without success.

This is not the type of homosexual that the police generally meet. They know the homosexual as the predatory man who loiters in public men's rooms. Or they see the man who compulsively seeks a quick partner in the park.

The Kinsey Report

The Hollywood House set, the Mattachine Society intellectual and the restroom habitué are the small visible layer of the iceberg of homosexuality in Washington.

No one knows how many homosexuals there are here, or in the United States. No one has taken a census of homosexuals.

Sixteen years ago, Alfred C. Kinsey published his famous study on "Sexual Behavior in the Human Male." The public was shocked by his figures on the incidence of homosexuality—and adultery and premarital sex and prostitution.

The homosexuals point to Kinsey's findings to back up their claim that they are the "Nation's second largest minority after the

Negro." They say there are 15 million homosexuals in the United States, ten per cent of the non-juvenile population.

More detached observers strongly dispute this figure. They think Kinsey's statistics (they measure homosexual behavior, not necessarily the number of "homosexuals") often are misused to inflate the size of the homosexual community. And in professional circles, there has been skepticism about Kinsey's sample. Some critics have speculated that homosexuals rushed to volunteer their case histories and distorted the findings.

Experts who venture an educated guess estimate homosexuals make up about 2 per cent of the adult male population. That would be about 1.2 million.

In Washington, taking the 1960 census count of 622,500 males 18 and up, it comes to about 12,500. New York and San Francisco may have more than the allotted 2 per cent because homosexuals are attracted to their "gay" communities. One "conservative" estimate for New York has been 100,000.

Numbers Game

For his report, Kinsey studied the case histories of 5300 white males. From these, he concluded that 4 per cent of males are exclusively homosexual throughout their lives.

But his other generalizations were more shocking to the public and have led to a numbers game of "1-in-6" and "1-in-3."

The Kinsey research team found that 37 per cent ("nearly 2 males out of every 5 that one may meet") have at least some overt homosexual experience to the point of orgasm between adolescence and old age. And 18 per cent (1-in-6) have at least as much of the homosexual as the heterosexual in their histories for at least three years between 16 and 55. This includes erotic reactions as well as overt acts. Ten per cent (1-in-10) are more or less exclusively homosexual for three adult years.

In a later study, Kinsey estimated that 3 per cent of adult females are exclusively homosexual.

One of Kinsey's severest critics was Dr. Edmund Bergler, a psychoanalyst. He felt that Kinsey's statistics could be dangerous because they made homosexual behavior "statistically acceptable." He spoke to young "borderline" recruits who might justify experimenting this way: "Why shouldn't I if every man in three that I meet on the street has had some homosexual experience?"

Kinsey's view was that homosexuality is neither abnormal nor unnatural. He saw it as a variant of sexual behavior for a minority and not as a symptom of an emotional disorder.

But this view is challenged by a growing school, notably among the psychoanalysts, that approaches homosexuality as a "disease" or "illness" in layman's language. Medical men prefer to use such terms as emotional disorder, psychopathologic condition, personality aberration or arrest of psychosexual development.

State of Mind

Whether or not homosexuality is considered a disease, the general belief today is that it is psychological in origin and not inherited. It is a state of mind rather than a state of body.

But there is not unanimity of opinions about the causes. Different studies have stressed different psychological patterns. The majority opinion points the finger at family environment, especially the parent-child relationship.

Last year, in a special report on homosexuality, the New York Academy of Medicine called on the medical profession to state its position on homosexuality and what can be done about it.

"Yet relatively little has been published about it in the medical and health journals, and there have been still fewer authoritative statements of position," the report noted.

In the legal as well as the medical profession, increasing attention is being given to the problem of homosexuality. Spokesmen for civil liberties groups have pointed out that many of our laws still carry the words of the English statute enacted under Henry

VIII and refer to "the abominable and detestable crime against nature."

Eight years ago the Wolfenden Report (produced by a committee headed by Sir John Wolfenden set up to advise the British Parliament on laws governing homosexual offenses and prostitution) recommended that homosexual acts between consenting adults in private should no longer be considered a crime.

In 1961, Illinois adopted a similar provision from the model code of the American Law Institute. The New York State Legislature soon will consider a similar recommendation from a special committee.

Society also is beginning to reexamine its attitudes as well as its laws on homosexuality.

Thirty years ago another social problem—venereal disease—also was conveniently ignored. Then Surgeon General Thomas Parran started a national crusade of public education to bring syphilis and other venereal diseases under control.

He brought the problem out into the open—the first step toward a more enlightened public attitude.

MONDAY: Freud's letter to a mother.

The Washington Post

Monday, Feb. 1, 1965

Those Others – II

Scientists Disagree on Basic Nature of Homosexuality, Chance of Cure

By Jean M. White

Washington Post Staff Writer

In April, 1935, Sigmund Freud answered a letter written him by a mother concerned about her son. He was understanding and kind but went directly to the point:

"I gather from your letter that your son is a homosexual. I am most impressed by the fact that you do not mention this term yourself in your information about him. May I question you, why do you avoid it?"

Homosexuality, Freud told the worried mother, is "assuredly no advantage" but neither, he added, is it a vice, crime, or degradation. He termed it "a variation of the sexual function produced by a certain arrest of sexual development."

As for treatment, Freud wrote that he could offer no prediction on a change to normal heterosexuality. But, he concluded:

"If he is unhappy, neurotic, torn by conflicts, inhibited in his social life, analysis may bring him harmony, peace of mind, full efficiency, whether he remains a homosexual or gets changed."

Freud's letter touches on basic questions that still produce sharp conflicts of opinion among reputable scientists when they discuss the nature of homosexuality.

What are the causes? Is it an illness? Can it be treated? Should a change be attempted? What should society do about it?

There is much that science does not know about homosexuality. But studies that have been made provide some enlightenment in the search for answers.

The most recent rigorous study was made by a special research team of the Society of Medical Psychoanalysts headed by Dr, Iving Bieber, associate clinical professor of psychiatry at New York Medical College. Over a nine-year period, the researchers compared 106 male homosexuals with 100 heterosexuals, all under treatment with 77 psychoanalysts of the Society.

In 1962, the conclusions were published in a thick volume entitled "Homosexuality: A Psychoanalytic Study of Male Homosexuals."

One of the cardinal findings of this study is that homosexuals are not born that way but become so because of problems in the parent-child relationship—typically a domineering mother and a cold, detached father.

This pattern of parental behavior produces incapacitating fears of the opposite sex. Blocked from the normal sexual outlet with women, the homosexual son has to seek substitute gratification with partners of his own sex.

The mother usually has a "close-binding-intimate" relationship with her son and is frequently seductive with him. She allies with him against his father and separates father from son.

The young boy's masculinity is smothered by his overprotective, overly intimate, excessively possessive mother. She does not encourage, and very frequently discourages, roughhouse sports with other boys. She may be harshly punitive when her son shows childhood sexual interest in girls, and she subtly disrupts adolescent dating attempts.

Father Is Key

And what about the father? He is generally detached, unaffectionate to his son, though he may have normal, positive attitudes toward his other sons. In many cases, he may be hostile to his pre-homosexual son.

Bieber sees the father as the key to whether a boy takes the homosexual path. A warm, affectionate father can neutralize the effects of the mother.

The majority of patients in the study group began their homosexual experiences with boys near their own age. Dr. Bieber doesn't feel seduction by an older man plays a significant role in turning boys toward homosexuality. The predisposing factors must be there if a brief episode—say an approach at a movie theater—is to have lasting effects.

In an interview recently, Dr. Bieber expanded his views:

"It's not easy to make a homosexual. You start with an organism that is built for heterosexual mating. Yet homosexuals like to say 'we're just like everyone else except for sexual preference'—it's a choice...

"They like to think that it's that way but it isn't. It's a substitute—abnormal adaptation—because they are afraid of heterosexual relations. They don't have a choice because of crippling fears."

Differing Views

Wardell B. Pomeroy, associate psychologist and coauthor of the Kinsey report, flatly disagrees with Dr. Bieber and the core of psychoanalytic theory that views homosexuality as a pathologic condition.

"A man can be a homosexual and not be emotionally disturbed," he maintains. "I know many happy homosexuals who are leading well-adjusted, socially productive lives. By any other criteria, they are normal."

Now a New York marriage counselor, Pomeroy pointed out in an interview that psychoanalysts see only maladjusted, disturbed homosexuals who come to them for treatment. He repeats the story about the analyst who was told by a colleague that all the colleague's homosexual patients were ill and replied: "So are all my heterosexual patients."

"I'd be the first to admit that there is a higher percentage of neurotics among homosexuals," Pomeroy says. "But this is largely due to society's pressure on them."

One of the chief arguments against the family-environment approach is that many boys do not become homosexuals even though they come from unhealthy home situations similar to those that produce the homosexual.

The answer may be that other favorable circumstances can break the homosexual pattern—an older brother or relative who offers a male image, for instance. Also a boy without strong sex drives may not pursue homosexual tendencies because of cultural pressures.

Natural Variant?

Pomeroy agrees with Kinsey and other investigators who think homosexuality is a natural variant of sexual behavior. Children begin with indiscriminate sex impulses that somewhere along the line are channeled into homosexuality by circumstances.

Perhaps a boy, developing strong sex drives in puberty, is blocked by society's strictures from heterosexual relations with girls. Perhaps he is awkward, stammers, is shy with girls. He may find an early experience with another boy gives him pleasure.

Thus, because of inhibitions and early experiences a boy may come to choose male sex partners. It may not be a free choice or preference, Pomeroy concedes, but then asks:

"But how many times do any of us have free choice, unlimited by circumstances?"

One factor that complicates any easy definition or simple approach to homosexuality is that it is not an "all or nothing" proposition.

There are gradations in sexuality from dominant homosexuality to dominant heterosexuality.

Kinsey drew up a seven-point scale from 0 (exclusively heterosexual) to 6 (exclusively homosexual). His 2s respond more strongly to the opposite sex but also are aroused by homosexual stimuli, whether or not carried through to overt acts. The 3s are equally homosexual or heterosexual in reaction and/or experiences.

Many medical men prefer not to use the term “bisexual” since it conjures up a half-female, half-male person. Some also think “latent homosexuality’ is an overworked term. In the same way, for instance, every homosexual could be said to have “latent heterosexuality.”

A report issued in 1955 by a committee of the Group for the Advancement of Psychiatry (GAP) states:

“Remnants of homosexual impulses from childhood exist in everyone. The average individual is usually not conscious of these feelings and reacts with disgust or revulsion toward the thought of any such impulses in themselves or others.”

Some persons can find satisfaction in relations with both sexes (the 2s, 3s, and 4s on the Kinsey scale). Some homosexuals marry, have children, and make an apparent success of marriage. Their wives may be unaware of the homosexual problem.

Double Lives

They may lead double lives as part-time homosexuals, going out for an occasional secret fling. Others may suppress their homosexual impulses until they lose control under some stress.

Dr. Edmund Bergler didn’t think much of such marriages. “Counterfeit sex” and “alibi marriages” was the way he characterized them and said they were used as cover by true homosexuals.

Many of the studies on homosexuality have been made among patients under treatment or men in prison. This has been a point of challenge by those who do not hold to the view that homosexuality is necessarily an emotional disorder.

They like to cite a study by Evelyn Hooker, a Los Angeles psychologist. She took 30 apparently well-adjusted homosexuals and matched them with 30 heterosexuals for age, education, and I.Q. She gave both groups a battery of tests and turned the results, unidentified, over to colleagues. They were unable to pick out the homosexuals with certainty.

Dr. Bieber speculates that this shows the tests are inadequate rather than homosexuals are emotionally healthy.

In its report to the British Parliament, the Wolfenden committee said it didn't feel that the witnesses had presented conclusive evidence to establish homosexuality as a disease.

People behave in many strange, unorthodox and socially unacceptable ways, the committee observed. But this doesn't necessarily mean they are ill, and homosexuality in many cases is the only symptom and is "compatible with full mental health in other respects."

But in a special report last year, the New York Academy of Medicine stated without qualification that homosexuality is a disease. As such, "it may be treated with improvement and success in some cases," the report added.

Up to now, there has been only limited success reported in treating homosexuals for a change. And therapy has been long and difficult.

First, the patient must want to change. Many homosexuals don't—they would rather fight than switch. They don't see themselves as sick or abnormal. The fault lies with society, not themselves. It is a matter of choice, preference. Or it is a congenital condition that can't be cured.

One New York homosexual made a poll of 300 colleagues. They were asked if they would change if there were an easy way, something like taking a pill. Ninety-seven per cent answered that they wouldn't change. But 83 per cent said they would not want their sons to be homosexuals.

One of the most optimistic reports of treatment for change comes from Dr. Bieber's study. He reported that 27 per cent "crossed over" to heterosexual orientation. But it took lengthy therapy, for most more than 350 sessions. This is not unusual, since therapy usually extends over two to four years.

At a meeting of the American Group Psychotherapy Association last week, a Philadelphia psychotherapist said homosexuality can be cured and warned that "propaganda" that it cannot should be actively opposed.

Dr. Samuel B. Hadden said he has been achieving good results since he began employing group psychotherapy ten years ago. All-homosexual groups work best, he explained, because the patients do not have to face the hostility that may drive them from mixed groups. The patient's rationalization that he is happy in his homosexuality is punctured when other members question his happiness.

Many psychoanalysts feel that homosexuals who are reasonably well adjusted in society should not be forced to attempt a change.

When success is so limited, adjustment often can be preferable to a cure. There is always the chance that the fears behind homosexual behavior are so strong the patient will be sent into an emotional tail-spin more disruptive of his life than homosexuality itself.

It such cases, analysts use therapy to allay anxieties and help develop self-control so that the homosexual won't some into conflict with law and society.

NEXT: The homosexual in society.

The Washington Post

Tuesday February 2, 1965

Those Others – III

Homosexuals Are in All Kinds of Jobs, Find Place in Many Levels of Society

By Jean M. White

Washington Post Staff Writer

"The main point is that we are like anyone else except in the area of sexual orientation."

The speaker was a well-built young man, masculine in appearance and manner.

Clark P. Polak, of Philadelphia, president of the Janus Society, was talking with reporters at a press conference called by ECHO (East Coast Homophile Organizations) during a three-day meeting at the Sheraton-Park Hotel last October. Close to a hundred homosexuals were registered for discussions on civil liberties and social rights.

"If someone came through the door now," Polak told the reporters, "I bet you couldn't tell whether he was one of us."

The reporters looked around the circle—and then were quick to stress their professional affiliation when anyone did come into the room.

Those who think they can spot a homosexual every time usually are wrong.

The "limp wrist" stereotype—mincing walk, swish, high-pitched voice—may hold true in the case of the obvious male homosexuals. But they are only the few. (And, the "butch" Lesbian, with her short hair and mannish dress, is the exception).

Some male homosexuals are athletic and virile-looking with out a trace of femininity.

On the West Coast, particularly, there is a sect of "he-men" homosexuals. They are partial to leather jackets and motorcycles and put a premium on rugged masculinity.

Some psychiatrists recognize that certain physical characteristics may be one factor in the homosexual pattern.

A frail boy with poor muscular co-ordination who can't throw a ball well is called a "sissy." He may withdraw from the competitive world of boys and find his way into homosexuality if other circumstances fit the pattern.

The homosexual is found in all types of jobs and professions—truck drivers, doctors, actors, salesmen, ditchdiggers, engineers, athletes and psychoanalysts.

It is true, however, that homosexuals seem to cluster around certain "arty" professions—the fashion industry, hairdressing, the theater and entertainment world. In fact, there seems to be some basis for the charge of "reverse discrimination"—that homosexuals hire their own kind and set up a "homosexual closed shop."

Insidious Underground

One psychoanalyst, Dr. Edmund Bergler, saw a kind of insidious underground at work in the fashion industry. Women, he warned, are being dressed by their worst enemies.

The claim has been made that homosexuals are more sensitive and creative than normal men. Homosexuals proudly point to Plato, Michelangelo, Tchaikovsky, Proust, Walt Whitman, and others. But the heterosexual list of talent and genius is far, far longer. And like their heterosexual brothers, homosexuals also wash dishes and run elevators.

Homosexuals probably have more time than most men to cultivate the arts of writing, drawing, and witty talk. They invest less time and energy in male sports and hobbies and are free of the responsibilities of marriage and parenthood.

By Sex Possessed

One thing psychiatrists have discovered is that the homosexual is likely to be far more preoccupied and obsessed with the topic of sex than most people.

Wardell B. Pomeroy, co-author of the Kinsey report and often a spokesman for homosexual causes, recognizes this.

"One problem is that the homosexual is obsessed, consumed by sex," he says. "Other men can sit around and talk about sports and politics. Not the homosexual."

One widely-held misconception is that all homosexuals hate women and avoid their company.

Actually, many homosexuals enjoy female companionship, although they fear women as sex partners. They often choose jobs where they can be in safe association with women. However, many Lesbians actively dislike men and regard them as superfluous in their lives.

Some psychiatrists have speculated that homosexuals often are stimulated by women and then take flight into homosexuality. A homosexual may go to dinner with a girl, say goodbye to her at the door, and then seek a male sex partner.

Homosexuals can have warm, tender feelings. Many want a stable, long-lasting relationship and search for the right male partner to share their lives.

Yet, their lives are usually a series of passing liaisons at the best. At worst, it consists of one-night stands, the pick-ups at a "fruit-stand" or "cruisy" bar.

The rules and practices of society tend to keep a man-woman marriage together even in the face of deep incompatibility. But society pressures tend to break up the homosexual couple. Without a community of interest centered on family and home, homosexual "marriages" are not likely to survive the first disagreement.

Because there are few long-term affairs, male homosexuals are forced to be promiscuous in their sex life.

Competitive Market

The homosexual seeks partners in a highly competitive sex market. Youth is prized in the "gay" world, and many male homosexuals pass into middle age to find they have to turn more and more to male prostitutes if they haven't become established in a private clique.

There are some psychoanalysts who feel homosexuals are emotionally ill and yet concede there can be a positive side in their finding a substitute, though a poor substitute, to fill the need for close human relationships.

Dr. Clara Thompson, once wrote:

"A homosexual way of life can play a constructive or destructive role in personality. It may be the best type of human relationship of which a person is capable and as such is better than isolation...Or it may be an added touch to an already deteriorating personality."

Health Danger

The homosexual's promiscuous sex life with changing partners has given rise to a serious public health problem in the control of venereal disease.

In some cities, nearly 50 per cent of those who come to public clinics admit homosexual contacts. Public health authorities now see the homosexual rivaling the prostitute as a VD carrier. Dr. C. Wendell Freeman, chief of the District's venereal disease control division, calls homosexual VD a "definite and serious problem" in Washington.

The Mattachine Society of Washington, which has 40 members, has tried to tackle the problem.

Mattachine leaders worked with health department officials in putting out and distributing a pamphlet on "Homosexuality and Venereal Disease." It promises records will be kept confidential and no information will be passed onto police.

Social Problems

Homosexuality does create some obvious social problems—venereal disease, flagrant solicitation in parks, the noisy, boisterous fringe that flowers in "pansy patches" and "petticoat lanes."

But on the whole, homosexuals are quiet and unobtrusive, more likely to be victimized than to do violence to others.

"Homosexuality isn't disruptive of society. It's more disruptive of the lives of the men involved," Dr. Bieber says.

On 42d Street off Times Square, male hoods prey on homosexuals, lead them on, and then rob and beat them up. Often a man will react to a homosexual advance with violence.

At times, it seems, the homosexual is his own worst enemy.

The "professional homosexual" who makes a career of militant homosexuality can come up with some bizarre causes.

Some speak of a "noble, superior way of life" as if they have found their own great society. Others push homosexuality as the answer to the population explosion. One homophile magazine contributor campaigned for the right to adopt children.

Homosexuality also can produce some rather bizarre situations, at least from society's point of view.

One of Washington's married homosexuals recently left his wife for a man. The two set up housekeeping, and the homosexual father took his two school-age children with him.

The cause of the homosexual also isn't helped by the obviously sick types—the transvestite "queens," the compulsive sex psychopaths, and the "sadie-mashies" (sadists-masochists). These are as unwelcome in polite "gay" society as child molesters and rapists are in straight heterosexual society.

The Difficult Life

Society makes life difficult for any homosexual, no matter how law-abiding he is. His whole life can crumble to ruin because of exposure.

Homosexuals see themselves as victims of social prejudice, an "unrecognized minority" suffering discrimination much like the Jews and Negroes) "only we have less visibility," one observed.

Franklin E. Kameny, president of the local Mattachine Society, says the homosexual seeks only equality in the eyes of the law and society.

"Why should society ask us to change?" he said. "You don't ask a Jew to change because there is anti-Semitism in the world."

Next: The homosexual and the law.

The Washington Post

Wednesday February 3, 1965

Those Others – IV

49 States and the District Punish Overt Homosexual Acts as Crimes

By Jean M. White

Washington Post Staff Writer

There has been much "cry Wolfenden" since the British Parliament received the report of a special commission eight years ago.

The commission, headed by Sir John Wolfenden, recommended that homosexual acts between consenting adults in private should no longer be regarded as a crime.

The British Parliament debated but never adopted the Wolfenden report recommendation.

In 1961, Illinois became the first State to exempt such homosexual acts from legal penalty. The New York State legislature soon will receive a similar recommendation from a commission set up to study revision of the State's criminal code.

In 49 states and the District of Columbia, an overt homosexual act is legally punishable under various statutes.

Most of these can be traced back to English common law and the sodomy statute in 1533 under Henry VIII, which referred to one type of homosexual act as "the abominable and detestable crime against nature, not to be named among Christians."

Actually, there is no law against being a homosexual. Homosexual acts generally fall under the loose heading of sodomy, which, under various state laws, covers a wide range of "unnatural" sex activity, with animals or persons of either sex, both within and outside marriage.

Penalties for sodomy can range from a minimum one-year prison sentence to North Carolina's maximum of 60 years.

In one recent case, a North Carolina defendant had been sentenced to 20 to 30 years in prison for a homosexual act involving consenting adults. A United States district judge ordered a new trial because the defendant had been deprived of full rights of counsel.

Then, going beyond this legal question, Judge James B. Craven was moved to ask:

"Is it not time to redraft a criminal statute first enacted in 1533? And if so, cannot the criminal law draftsmen be helped by those best informed on the subject—medical doctors—in attempting to classify offenders? Is there any public purpose served by a possible 60-year maximum or even a 5-year minimum imprisonment of the occasional or one-time homosexual, without treatment, and if so, what is it?"

Experts at Odds

The American Law Institute, which in 1955 drew up a model code that omitted private, voluntary homosexual acts between adults, has observed that experts on homosexuality are in such disagreement as to cause and possible treatment that "the lawmaker must proceed cautiously in decreeing drastic measures..."

Many medical and legal experts feel our present homosexual laws already are "drastic" and also antiquated and unenforceable.

They argue that the law should draw a line between anti-social behavior that is dangerous (child molestation, public indecency, acts by force) and those acts carried out discreetly by adults. They raise the fundamental question of the protection to which an individual is entitled against state interference in his personal affairs when he is not hurting others or the public good.

Not the Law's Business

The Wolfenden report put it this way:

"Unless a deliberate attempt is to be made by society...to equate the sphere of crime with that of sin, there must remain a realm of private morality and immorality which is, in brief and crude terms, not the law's business."

As for opening "the floodgates to unbridled license," the Wolfenden commission wryly observed that "the expectation seems to us to exaggerate the effect of law on human behavior."

In European countries that do not punish private homosexual acts, the commission noted, it could find no evidence of an appreciable increase in homosexuality or large-scale proselytizing. The question is whether any man who finds homosexual behavior repugnant will find it less repugnant if the law doesn't punish it.

Feelings of Disgust

Homosexuality raises such feelings of distaste, even disgust, that dispassionate discussion of law changes is often impossible.

These feelings are deeply rooted in the Judeo-Christian ethic and tied to fear of legalizing immorality. In recent years, however, a number of church statements have taken note of modern psychiatric and sociological views.

Still the legal-religious debate goes on. A spokesman for the Catholic Church, appearing at a public hearing on the proposed revisions of New York's legal code, termed homosexuality "an increasing threat to sound family planning in our community." An Episcopal Church representative, however, spoke of an enlightened advance over existing laws.

"Towards a Quaker View of Sex," a statement prepared by a group of British Quakers in 1963, suggested that society "should no more deplore homosexuality than left-handedness," although it can prohibit certain types of behavior.

Man's Responsibility

A basic legal question is a man's responsibility for his acts. The Wolfenden commission refused to accept homosexuality as a disease that the sufferer cannot help, for this carries the implication of "diminished responsibility."

Members of society, the report emphasizes, have to practice some measure of self-control in daily experience. A person tries to control coughing at a concert. And a man must act with restraint upon seeing a pretty girl on the street.

Despite the "cry Wolfenden," it is not in the area of private acts that the homosexual often comes into conflict with the law as it is practiced.

The statutory laws against such acts are chiefly a pressure point for blackmail and extortion rather than an area for law enforcement. This probably is not so much a matter of principle as of practicality.

In most cases, it is difficult for police to obtain evidence of illegal sexual acts performed in private.

It is in the area of public "solicitation" that the homosexual generally runs into trouble with the police.

Few Lasting Attachments

Male homosexuals form few lasting attachments. They constantly are seeking new sex partners in "cruising" forays. Perhaps two strangers meet in a park, and one invites the other to his apartment. The rendezvous negotiation is observed by a policeman. Or the park pickup may turn out to be a morals squad officer.

The encounter ends with an arrest on the charge of disorderly conduct. On the police books in Washington, the charge is repeated—disorderly conduct (indecent gestures); disorderly conduct (loitering); disorderly conduct (soliciting).

Most defendants forfeit $25 to $100, and the cases do not come to trial. For a charge of sodomy (10 years in prison or $1000 fine), a homosexual must be caught in the overt act. Such an arrest is rare.

"Decoys" Assailed

Civil libertarians have questioned the limits of proper police enforcement in pursuing homosexual offenders.

They attack the use of "peep holes" for secret surveillance of public restrooms and charge policemen are used as decoys to "entice" homosexuals by actively inviting a homosexual advance as a basis for arrest.

The homosexual himself complains that he is hounded by police and prevented from making the romantic overtures allowed heterosexuals. The homosexual may overstate his case somewhat. Dr. Irving Bieber, a New York psychoanalyst and author of a recent study on homosexuality, feels that homosexuals often overstep the bounds of good taste and go beyond the acceptable boy-girl dating techniques.

Whether this is true or not, lawyers in the field of civil liberties still are disturbed by certain police tactics.

The National Capital Area Civil Liberties Union has written the District Commissioners to protest against "peep hole" surveillance and the use of police decoys in civilian clothes to apprehend sex offenders. The use of "peep holes," the statement emphasized, is "an unreasonable invasion of the privacy of all members of the public who use" the facilities.

Uniformed Police Urged

The Civil Liberties Union argued that right of the public to be free of solicitation and annoyance would be better secured by patrols of uniformed policemen than by secret peeking and "enticement of a special undercover squad."

Soon afterwards, District officials urged several local establishments in which 191 sex arrests had been made over the period of a year to employ attendants to supervise their men's rooms.

The police defend their practices and feel they have been unjustly branded by such catch words as "enticement" and "entrapment."

This is how one veteran police officer sums up the case for the police:

"People can't understand a problem they don't see. We see them—these men are predatory. They hang around theaters, store, and public restrooms. It is a question of public decency. We're not interested in the non-predatory ones or acts in private.

"What about the danger to youngsters who see this or are molested. You get a call from a Midwest Senator with a parent's complaint about what his son saw on a high-school trip to Washington."

Police Defended

Another veteran police officer further defends police practices as a means of preventing murder growing out of homosexual trysts.

Accounts that morals squad officers spend hours peering through peep holes rouse police wrath and indignation.

"Our officers may go in for five or ten minutes and then leave to come back again for a short time hours later," a police official protested. "They don't sit by hours at peep holes. They don't have the time."

There are four plainclothesmen assigned to the morals squad. At police headquarters, their appearance is that of clean-cut men with normal clothes and haircuts. In the past, there were complaints that morals squad men "camped it up"—dressed and acted like stereotyped homosexuals to tempt suspects and provoke advances.

Homosexuals point out that many personal tragedies occur not so much because of the arrest itself but because of the disclosure of information to Government agencies.

Cause for Dismissal

The Federal Government views homosexuality as sufficient cause for job dismissal.

A case recently reported in the New Republic in an article by James Ridgeway involved a Government employee of 15 years with a GS-14 rank.

The Federal employee had been arrested by police who trailed two men to an apartment house parking lot after observing a curbstone conversation near Lafayette Park when a car stopped. The two were given speeding summonses and released. But the security chief for the National Aeronautics and Space Administration had been called by police and proceeded to interview the NASA employee.

The upshot was that the NASA employee was later dismissed from his job. He is contesting the dismissal in court.

To the law, the homosexual offender may be a confirmed, casual, or even one-time homosexual. All are equal in having been caught in the act. The background of the offender makes no difference.

In many cities, police allow "gay" bars to operate as a way to keep tabs on the homosexual community. One problem for police is to protect the homosexual himself—he often is prey to hoods and the victim of violence in sex slayings.

In one area at least, homosexuals have praise for the Washington police. The Mattachine Society says it has an agreement for homosexuals to report blackmail attempts to police without fear of prosecution themselves.

Beyond the law, homosexuals still must face social hostility. Donald Webster Cory, a married homosexual who writes under a pseudonym and has become a semi-official spokesman for the homosexual community, recognizes this.

In "The Homosexual in America," he wrote:

"Whether organized society passes laws and enforces them, or effaces such laws from its statute books, is important, although secondary to social condemnation."

Next: Jobs and security for the homosexual.

Jobs

The Washington Post

Thursday February 4, 1965

Those Others – V

Homosexuals' Militancy Reflected in Attacks on Ouster from U.S. Jobs

Last of five articles

By Jean M. White

Washington Post Staff Writer

When a public hearing on job discrimination was held in Washington two years ago, the Mattachine Society submitted a statement protesting discrimination against homosexuals in both public and private employment.

The homosexual pictures himself as a member of a true minority group suffering unreasonable discrimination and social prejudice.

His situation, he says, is even worse than that of the Negro because he has to fight the active hostility of the Federal Government. Among his complaints are these:

He can't hold a Government job. He can't get security clearance. He can't serve his country in the armed forces. His choice, as he sees it, it either to lie or to be an outcast in society with neither the duties not the rights of other citizens.

At times the homosexual may have such all-absorbing preoccupation with his plight that he fails to face up to the realities of the society in which he must live. Whether right or wrong, society's hostility does exist.

But one fact is undeniable; with few exceptions, only the fact the homosexuals are not known to their employers prevents the entire group from being unemployed.

In recent years, there has been a spate of court cases attacking the Federal Government's policies on employment of homosexuals. This reflects both the homosexual's more militant stance and the concern of civil libertarians for individual rights.

The cases point up the tangled issues and the danger of making sweeping generalizations where homosexuality is concerned.

One case involves the dismissal of a Federal Aviation Agency clerk for four isolated homosexual acts in his youth at a small Southern college. The evidence showed no repetition, and normal sex life since 1950, with marriage and three children.

Here the issue is dismissal based on the grounds of isolated homosexual experiences in an employee's remote and youthful past. In this case, the FAA clerk was reinstated with back pay soon after the Supreme Court agreed to review the suit.

Another legal challenge to Civil Service Commission policies has come in a suit filed by a former Government employee who reapplied for a job with the Labor Department. He passed three competitive CSC exams for personnel jobs. But he was disqualified when a check turned up information that he was a homosexual.

Dismissal Contested

Here the issue is automatic disqualification of an admitted homosexual, who maintains his private sex life has nothing to do with job performance. The Court of Appeals is expected to rule on this case within a few weeks.

In still another case, a meteorologist was fired from his nonsensitive GS-14 job with the National Aeronautics and Space Administration. The basis for discharge came from interrogations by NASA security officers who were notified by Police Headquarters. Police had picked up the NASA employee but apparently didn't find enough evidence to press a charge of homosexual behavior. CSC discharge hearings have less rigorous rules of procedure and evidence than do courts. A supervisor testified the employee's work was "very good" but his continued employment might be "embarrassing."

Here the employee is contesting dismissal on the grounds NASA security officials got their information after an illegal arrest without probable cause.

The policy of the Civil Service Commission can be summed up very simply: Homosexuals are unsuitable to hold Government jobs, sensitive or non-sensitive. Evidence of homosexual behavior is sufficient ground for dismissal as "immoral conduct."

1950 Probe Recalled

The Federal Government's stern attitude toward homosexuals is in part a reflex action after being badly burned during congressional investigations in the early 1950s.

In 1950, a Senate subcommittee was set up "to make an investigation into the employment by the Government of homosexuals and other sexual perverts." Lt. Roy E. Blick, then head of the District morals squad, had testified that his records showed 3750 "perverts" in the Government. Senate investigators then gave close attention and widespread publicity to the presence of "sex perverts on the public payroll," particularly in the State Department.

Last October, the National Capital Area Civil Liberties Union asked the CSC to end its policy of "automatic rejection of all homosexuals for all jobs in Government on that ground alone."

The Union made it clear that it is not contending that homosexuals are invariably good Federal employees. But, it emphasized, "there has been no proof to support the governmental assumption that they are all invariably bad Federal employees."

A man's private sex life bears no necessary relation to how he performs his job, the Union argues.

'Inflexible Rules' Decried

In 1955, the Committee on Cooperation with Governmental (Federal) Agencies of the Group for the Advancement of Psychiatry (GAP) made a report on homosexuality "with particular emphasis on this problem in government agencies."

One of its conclusions was this:

"In the governmental setting as well as in civilian life, homosexuals have functioned with distinction and without disruption of morale or efficiency. Problems of social maladaptive behavior, such as homosexuality, therefore need to be examined on an individual basis, considering the place and circumstances, rather than from inflexible rules."

The NCACLU would say that the Government now operates from "inflexible rules" when dealing with homosexuals.

Government's Reasons

The Government has three principle arguments to justify its policies: (1) homosexuality constitutes "immoral conduct" in our society; (2) presence of homosexuals disrupts morale and efficiency of coworkers; (3) homosexuals are security risks because they are emotionally unstable and vulnerable to blackmail.

Witnesses at discharge hearings often mention fear of scandal and the public's reaction to support a dismissal for homosexual conduct. A District Court judge upheld one discharge with the observation that "homosexual conduct is immoral under the present mores of our society and is abhorrent to the majority of people."

The Civil Liberties Union argues that the government shouldn't set itself up as the moral judge of the private sex life of adult employees if there is no proof of harm to the public.

As for the contention that homosexuals disrupt morale and efficiency, the Union maintains the CSC has yet to offer evidence that a homosexual upsets office efficiency and morale. A gossipy clerk or cranky secretary might do the same, and these crises are handled when they arise.

Listed as Security Risks

When security is involved, the question of homosexuals in Government jobs becomes the most controversial. There are those who will fight for a qualified homosexual's right to hold a non-sensitive position but reluctantly feel they must draw the line on sensitive jobs.

A 1953 Presidential Executive Order defines "security risks" to include sex perverts, heavy drinkers, loose talkers, and persons judged unreliable, untrustworthy, or immoral. It is interpreted as a bar to granting security clearances to homosexuals.

Intelligence and security officers say homosexuals present a special security hazard on two counts. First, they are prime targets for blackmailers. Second, they are emotionally immature and unstable, talk too much, and are highly susceptible to flattery.

The GAP committee noted that it had not found any material from a scientific study to support the view that weak moral fiber makes homosexuals more susceptible to the blandishments of foreign agents or more likely to break down under interrogations than any other group.

To those who point to blackmail, the homosexual asks: "What about the married man having an extramarital affair? Isn't he as vulnerable as we are?"

Involved in Espionage

In the last 15 years, there have been several widely publicized espionage cases involving suspected homosexuals—William John Vassall, the British Admiralty clerk; Guy Burgess and Donald MacLean, the British diplomats who fled to Russia, and William H. Martin and Bernon F. Mitchell, the National Security Agency code clerks who also turned up in Moscow.

But there also have been cases involving blonds, drunkards, and, most of all, avarice.

The National Capital Area Civil Liberties Union makes this comment:

"History is replete with instances where heterosexual behavior has led to serious difficulties, yet heterosexuals are not barred from Government employment."

Views on Blackmail

The Union argues that the Government's attitude toward the homosexual provides one of the chief pressure points for blackmail. He must hide his homosexual leanings or lose his job.

Beyond this, however, there is always the specter of social denunciation and ostracism. The blackmailer often works on his victim's fear of public exposure as well as the fear of job loss.

After the arrest of Walter W. Jenkins, a trusted White House aide, on a morals charge last October, the American Mental Health Foundation sent a letter to President Johnson deploring "the kind of hysteria that demands that all homosexual persons be barred from any responsible position." The fact that an individual is a homosexual, the statement stressed, does not "per se make him more unstable or more of a security risk than any heterosexual person."

A CSC spokesperson says that it does take into account an individual's background and might overlook isolated remote homosexual experience if a job applicant is "rehabilitated."

Barred by Military

The military branches actively weed out homosexuals from their ranks. Homosexuals protest indignantly that they have to lie if they want to serve their country. Draft eligibles are asked the question: Do you have any homosexual tendencies?

Many homosexuals have entered the armed forces and have gone undetected. Many have been good soldiers, and some have served with distinction.

Yet even sympathetic observers have expressed doubts about homosexuals in uniform. In "The Homosexual Revolution," R. E. L. Masters points out that, with present-day American attitudes, a prohibition should be understood as a military rather than a moral judgment, with practical reasons behind it. He compares the situation to that of a heterosexual male disguised as a female living in barracks of young women.

Unfairness Charged

But he protests against the unfairness of a situation where a man can be thrown out with a less-than-honorable discharge even after he has served faithfully without flagrant misconduct. Such a discharge carries a stigma into civilian life.

The public response to the Jenkins arrest has been encouraging of a more enlightened public attitude. On the whole, public comment showed restraint, decency, and compassion for the personal tragedy of a man and his family.

But today society offers no place, no help, and no hope to the homosexual. Laws are harsh on him; his existence is precarious; exposure brings ruin and social ostracism.

Yet society has to deal with the homosexual in its midst. And it will never be able to do this with fairness and compassion until it understands more about what has been called "the riddle of homosexuality."

The Speech

The speech by Martin Luther King, Jr. that Michael heard in Montgomery not only affected him, but it inspired countless numbers of people on that day and since.

Michael heard these words as a young gay man, and while he recognized the importance of the words as the speaker delivered them, he also applied them to his own life by substituting "heterosexual" for "white" and "homosexual" for "black" as he was listening. He concluded that homosexuals were deserving of the justice to which Dr. King referred.

Our God is Marching On!

March 25, 1965. Montgomery, AL

My dear and abiding friends, Ralph Abernathy, and to all of the distinguished Americans seated here on the rostrum, my friends and co-workers of the state of Alabama, and to all of the freedom-loving people who have assembled here this afternoon from all over our nation and from all over the world: Last Sunday, more than eight thousand of us started on a mighty walk from Selma, Alabama. We have walked through desolate valleys and across the trying hills. We have walked on meandering highways and rested our bodies on rocky byways. Some of our faces are burned from the outpourings of the sweltering sun. Some have literally slept in the mud. We have been drenched by the rains. [*Audience:*] (*Speak*) Our bodies are tired and our feet are somewhat sore.

But today as I stand before you and think back over that great march, I can say, as Sister Pollard said—a seventy-year-old Negro woman who lived in this community during the bus boycott—and one day, she was asked while walking if she didn't want to ride. And when she answered, "No," the person said, "Well, aren't you tired?" And with her ungrammatical profundity, she said, "My feets is tired, but my soul is rested." (*Yes, sir. All right*) And in a real sense this afternoon, we can say that our feet are tired, (*Yes, sir*) but our souls are rested.

They told us we wouldn't get here. And there were those who said that we would get here only over their dead bodies, (*Well. Yes, sir. Talk*) but all the world today knows that we are here and we are standing before the forces of power in the state of Alabama saying, "We ain't goin' let nobody turn us around." (*Yes, sir. Speak*) [*Applause*]

Now it is not an accident that one of the great marches of American history should terminate in Montgomery, Alabama. (*Yes, *sir)* Just ten years ago, in this very city, a new philosophy was born of the Negro struggle. Montgomery was the first city in the South in which the entire Negro community united and squarely faced its age-old oppressors. *(Yes, sir. Well)* Out of this struggle, more than bus [*de*]segregation was won; a new idea, more powerful than guns or clubs was born. Negroes took it and carried it across the South in epic battles *(Yes, sir. Speak)* that electrified the nation *(Well)* and the world.

Yet, strangely, the climactic conflicts always were fought and won on Alabama soil. After Montgomery's, heroic confrontations loomed up in Mississippi, Arkansas, Georgia, and elsewhere. But not until the colossus of segregation was challenged in Birmingham did the conscience of America begin to bleed. White America was profoundly aroused by Birmingham because it witnessed the whole community of Negroes facing terror and brutality with majestic scorn and heroic courage. And from the wells of this democratic spirit, the nation finally forced Congress *(Well)* to write legislation *(Yes, sir)* in the hope that it would eradicate the stain of Birmingham. The Civil Rights Act of 1964 gave Negroes some part of their rightful dignity, *(Speak, sir)* but without the vote it was dignity without strength. *(Yes, sir)*

Once more the method of nonviolent resistance *(Yes)* was unsheathed from its scabbard, and once again an entire community was mobilized to confront the adversary. *(Yes, sir)* And again the brutality of a dying order shrieks across the land. Yet, Selma, Alabama, became a shining moment in the conscience of man. If the worst in American life lurked in its dark streets, the best of American instincts arose passionately from across the nation to overcome it. *(Yes, sir. Speak)* There never was a moment in American history *(Yes, sir)* more honorable and more inspiring than the pilgrimage of clergymen and laymen of every race and faith pouring into Selma to face danger *(Yes)* at the side of its embattled Negroes.

The confrontation of good and evil compressed in the tiny community of Selma (*Speak, speak*) generated the massive power (*Yes, sir. Yes, sir*) to turn the whole nation to a new course. A president born in the South (*Well*) had the sensitivity to feel the will of the country, (*Speak, sir*) and in an address that will live in history as one of the most passionate pleas for human rights ever made by a president of our nation, he pledged the might of the federal government to cast off the centuries-old blight. President Johnson rightly praised the courage of the Negro for awakening the conscience of the nation. (*Yes, sir*)

On our part we must pay our profound respects to the white Americans who cherish their democratic traditions over the ugly customs and privileges of generations and come forth boldly to join hands with us. (*Yes, sir*) From Montgomery to Birmingham, (*Yes, sir*) from Birmingham to Selma, (*Yes, sir*) from Selma back to Montgomery, (*Yes*) a trail wound in a circle long and often bloody, yet it has become a highway up from darkness. (*Yes, sir*) Alabama has tried to nurture and defend evil, but evil is choking to death in the dusty roads and streets of this state. (*Yes, sir. Speak, sir*) So I stand before you this afternoon (*Speak, sir. Well*) with the conviction that segregation is on its deathbed in Alabama, and the only thing uncertain about it is how costly the segregationists and Wallace will make the funeral. (*Go ahead. Yes, sir*) [*Applause*]

Our whole campaign in Alabama has been centered around the right to vote. In focusing the attention of the nation and the world today on the flagrant denial of the right to vote, we are exposing the very origin, the root cause, of racial segregation in the Southland. Racial segregation as a way of life did not come about as a natural result of hatred between the races immediately after the Civil War. There were no laws segregating the races then. And as the noted historian, C. Vann Woodward, in his book, *The Strange Career of Jim Crow*, clearly points out, the segregation of the races was really a political stratagem employed by the emerging Bourbon interests in the South to keep the southern masses divided and southern labor the cheapest in the land. You see, it was a simple thing to keep the poor white masses working for near-starvation wages in the years that followed the Civil War. Why, if the poor white plantation or mill worker became dissatisfied with his low wages, the plantation or mill owner would merely threaten to fire him and hire former Negro slaves and pay him even less. Thus, the southern wage level was kept almost unbearably low.

Toward the end of the Reconstruction era, something very significant happened. (*Listen to him*) That is what was known as the Populist Movement. (*Speak, sir*) The leaders of this movement began awakening the poor white masses (*Yes, sir*) and the former Negro slaves to the fact that they were being fleeced by the emerging Bourbon interests. Not only that, but they began uniting the Negro and white masses (*Yeah*) into a voting bloc that threatened to drive the Bourbon interests from the command posts of political power in the South.

To meet this threat, the southern aristocracy began immediately to engineer this development of a segregated society. (*Right*) I want you to follow me through here because this is very important to see the roots of racism and the denial of the right to vote. Through their control of mass media, they revised the doctrine of white supremacy. They saturated the thinking of the poor white masses with it, (*Yes*) thus clouding their minds to the real issue involved in the Populist Movement. They then directed the placement on the books of the South of laws that made it a crime for Negroes and whites to come together as equals at any level. (*Yes, sir*) And that did it. That crippled and eventually destroyed the Populist Movement of the nineteenth century.

If it may be said of the slavery era that the white man took the world and gave the Negro Jesus, then it may be said of the Reconstruction era that the southern aristocracy took the world and gave the poor white man Jim Crow. (*Yes, sir*) He gave him Jim Crow. (*Uh huh*) And when his wrinkled stomach cried out for the food that his empty pockets could not provide, (*Yes, sir*) he ate Jim Crow, a psychological bird that told him that no matter how bad off he was, at least he was a white man, better than the black man. (*Right sir*) And he ate Jim Crow. (*Uh huh*) And when his undernourished children cried out for the necessities that his low wages could not provide, he showed them the Jim Crow signs on the buses and in the stores, on the streets and in the public buildings. (*Yes, sir*) And his children, too, learned to feed upon Jim Crow, (*Speak*) their last outpost of psychological oblivion. (*Yes, sir*)

Thus, the threat of the free exercise of the ballot by the Negro and the white masses alike (*Uh huh*) resulted in the establishment of a segregated society. They segregated southern money from the poor whites; they segregated southern mores from the rich whites; (*Yes, sir*) they segregated southern churches from Christianity (*Yes, sir*); they segregated southern minds from honest thinking; (*Yes, sir*) and they segregated the Negro from everything. (*Yes, sir*) That's what happened when the Negro and white masses of the South threatened to unite and build a great society: a society of justice where none would pray upon the weakness of others; a society of plenty where greed and poverty would be done away; a society of brotherhood where every man would respect the dignity and worth of human personality. (*Yes, sir*)

We've come a long way since that travesty of justice was perpetrated upon the American mind. James Weldon Johnson put it eloquently. He said:

We have come over a way
That with tears hath been watered. (*Yes, sir*)
We have come treading our paths
Through the blood of the slaughtered. (*Yes, sir*)

Out of the gloomy past, *(Yes, sir)*
Till now we stand at last
Where the white gleam
Of our bright star is cast. *(Speak, sir)*

Today I want to tell the city of Selma, *(Tell them, Doctor)* today I want to say to the state of Alabama, *(Yes, sir)* today I want to say to the people of America and the nations of the world, that we are not about to turn around. *(Yes, sir)* We are on the move now. *(Yes, sir)*

Yes, we are on the move and no wave of racism can stop us. *(Yes, sir)* We are on the move now. The burning of our churches will not deter us. *(Yes, sir)* The bombing of our homes will not dissuade us. *(Yes, sir)* We are on the move now. *(Yes, sir)* The beating and killing of our clergymen and young people will not divert us. We are on the move now. *(Yes, sir)* The wanton release of their known murderers would not discourage us. We are on the move now. *(Yes, sir)* Like an idea whose time has come, *(Yes, sir)* not even the marching of mighty armies can halt us. *(Yes, sir)* We are moving to the land of freedom. *(Yes, sir)*

Let us therefore continue our triumphant march *(Uh huh)* to the realization of the American dream. *(Yes, sir)* Let us march on segregated housing *(Yes, sir)* until every ghetto or social and economic depression dissolves, and Negroes and whites live side by side in decent, safe, and sanitary housing. *(Yes, sir)* Let us march on segregated schools *(Let us march, Tell it)* until every vestige of segregated and inferior education becomes a thing of the past, and Negroes and whites study side-by-side in the socially-healing context of the classroom.

Let us march on poverty *(Let us march)* until no American parent has to skip a meal so that their children may eat. *(Yes, sir)* March on poverty *(Let us march)* until no starved man walks the streets of our cities and towns *(Yes, sir)* in search of jobs that do not exist. *(Yes, sir)* Let us march on poverty *(Let us march)* until wrinkled stomachs in Mississippi are filled, *(That's right)* and the idle industries of Appalachia are realized and revitalized, and broken lives in sweltering ghettos are mended and remolded.

Let us march on ballot boxes, (*Let's march*) march on ballot boxes until race-baiters disappear from the political arena.

Let us march on ballot boxes until the salient misdeeds of bloodthirsty mobs (*Yes, sir*) will be transformed into the calculated good deeds of orderly citizens. (*Speak, Doctor*)

Let us march on ballot boxes (*Let us march*) until the Wallaces of our nation tremble away in silence.

Let us march on ballot boxes (*Let us march*) until we send to our city councils (*Yes, sir*), state legislatures, (*Yes, sir*) and the United States Congress, (*Yes, sir*) men who will not fear to do justly, love mercy, and walk humbly with thy God.

Let us march on ballot boxes (*Let us march. March*) until brotherhood becomes more than a meaningless word in an opening prayer, but the order of the day on every legislative agenda.

Let us march on ballot boxes (*Yes*) until all over Alabama God's children will be able to walk the earth in decency and honor.

There is nothing wrong with marching in this sense. (*Yes, sir*) The Bible tells us that the mighty men of Joshua merely walked about the walled city of Jericho (*Yes*) and the barriers to freedom came tumbling down. (*Yes, sir*) I like that old Negro spiritual, (*Yes, sir*) "Joshua Fit the Battle of Jericho." In its simple, yet colorful, depiction (*Yes, sir*) of that great moment in biblical history, it tells us that:

Joshua fit the battle of Jericho, (*Tell it*)
Joshua fit the battle of Jericho, (*Yes, sir*)
And the walls come tumbling down. (*Yes, sir. Tell it*)
Up to the walls of Jericho they marched, spear in hand. (*Yes, sir*)
"Go blow them ramhorns," Joshua cried,
"'Cause the battle am in my hand." (*Yes, sir*)

These words I have given you just as they were given us by the unknown, long-dead, dark-skinned originator. (*Yes, sir*) Some now long-gone black bard bequeathed to posterity these words in ungrammatical form, (*Yes, sir*) yet with emphatic pertinence for all of us today. (*Uh huh*)

The battle is in our hands. And we can answer with creative nonviolence the call to higher ground to which the new directions of our struggle summons us. (*Yes, sir*) The road ahead is not altogether a smooth one. (*No*) There are no broad highways that lead us easily and inevitably to quick solutions. But we must keep going.

In the glow of the lamplight on my desk a few nights ago, I gazed again upon the wondrous sign of our times, full of hope and promise of the future. (*Uh huh*) And I smiled to see in the newspaper photographs of many a decade ago, the faces so bright, so solemn, of our valiant heroes, the people of Montgomery. To this list may be added the names of all those (*Yes*) who have fought and, yes, died in the nonviolent army of our day: Medgar Evers, (*Speak*) three civil rights workers in Mississippi last summer, (*Uh huh*) William Moore, as has already been mentioned, (*Yes, sir*) the Reverend James Reeb, (*Yes, sir*) Jimmy Lee Jackson, (*Yes, sir*) and four little girls in the church of God in Birmingham on Sunday morning. (*Yes, sir*) But in spite of this, we must go on and be sure that they did not die in vain. (*Yes, sir*) The pattern of their feet as they walked through Jim Crow barriers in the great stride toward freedom is the thunder of the marching men of Joshua, (*Yes, sir*) and the world rocks beneath their tread. (*Yes, sir*)

My people, my people, listen. (*Yes, sir*) The battle is in our hands. (*Yes, sir*) The battle is in our hands in Mississippi and Alabama and all over the United States. (*Yes, sir*) I know there is a cry today in Alabama, (*Uh huh*) we see it in numerous editorials: "When will Martin Luther King, SCLC, SNCC, and all of these civil rights agitators and all of the white clergymen and labor leaders and students and others get out of our community and let Alabama return to normalcy?"

But I have a message that I would like to leave with Alabama this evening. (*Tell it*) That is exactly what we don't want, and we will

not allow it to happen, (*Yes, sir*) for we know that it was normalcy in Marion (*Yes, sir*) that led to the brutal murder of Jimmy Lee Jackson. (*Speak*) It was normalcy in Birmingham (*Yes*) that led to the murder on Sunday morning of four beautiful, unoffending, innocent girls. It was normalcy on Highway 80 (*Yes, sir*) that led state troopers to use tear gas and horses and billy clubs against unarmed human beings who were simply marching for justice. (*Speak, sir*) It was normalcy by a cafe in Selma, Alabama, that led to the brutal beating of Reverend James Reeb.

It is normalcy all over our country (*Yes, sir*) which leaves the Negro perishing on a lonely island of poverty in the midst of vast ocean of material prosperity. It is normalcy all over Alabama (*Yeah*) that prevents the Negro from becoming a registered voter. (*Yes*) No, we will not allow Alabama (*Go ahead*) to return to normalcy. [*Applause*]

The only normalcy that we will settle for (*Yes, sir*) is the normalcy that recognizes the dignity and worth of all of God's children. The only normalcy that we will settle for is the normalcy that allows judgment to run down like waters, and righteousness like a mighty stream. (*Yes, sir*) The only normalcy that we will settle for is the normalcy of brotherhood, the normalcy of true peace, the normalcy of justice.

And so as we go away this afternoon, let us go away more than ever before committed to this struggle and committed to nonviolence. I must admit to you that there are still some difficult days ahead. We are still in for a season of suffering in many of the black belt counties of Alabama, many areas of Mississippi, many areas of Louisiana. I must admit to you that there are still jail cells waiting for us, and dark and difficult moments. But if we will go on with the faith that nonviolence and its power can transform dark yesterdays into bright tomorrows, we will be able to change all of these conditions.

And so I plead with you this afternoon as we go ahead: remain committed to nonviolence. Our aim must never be to defeat or humiliate the white man, but to win his friendship and understanding. We must come to see that the end we seek is a society at peace with itself, a society that can live with its conscience. And that will be a day not of the white man, not of the black man. That will be the day of man as man. (*Yes*)

I know you are asking today, "How long will it take?" (*Speak, sir*) Somebody's asking, "How long will prejudice blind the visions of men, darken their understanding, and drive bright-eyed wisdom from her sacred throne?" Somebody's asking, "When will wounded justice, lying prostrate on the streets of Selma and Birmingham and communities all over the South, be lifted from this dust of shame to reign supreme among the children of men?" Somebody's asking, "When will the radiant star of hope be plunged against the nocturnal bosom of this lonely night, (*Speak, speak, speak*) plucked from weary souls with chains of fear and the manacles of death? How long will justice be crucified, (*Speak*) and truth bear it?" (*Yes, sir*)

I come to say to you this afternoon, however difficult the moment, (*Yes, sir*) however frustrating the hour, it will not be long, (*No sir*) because "truth crushed to earth will rise again." (*Yes, sir*)

How long? Not long, (*Yes, sir*) because "no lie can live forever." (*Yes, sir*)

How long? Not long, (*All right. How long*) because "you shall reap what you sow." (*Yes, sir*)

How long? (*How long?*) Not long: (*Not long*)
Truth forever on the scaffold, (*Speak*)
Wrong forever on the throne, (*Yes, sir*)
Yet that scaffold sways the future, (*Yes, sir*)
And, behind the dim unknown,
Standeth God within the shadow,
Keeping watch above his own.

How long? Not long, because the arc of the moral universe is long, but it bends toward justice. (*Yes, sir*)

How long? Not long, (*Not long*) because:

Mine eyes have seen the glory of the coming of the Lord; (*Yes, sir*)

He is trampling out the vintage where the grapes of wrath are stored; (*Yes*)

He has loosed the fateful lightning of his terrible swift sword; (*Yes, sir*)

His truth is marching on. (*Yes, sir*)

He has sounded forth the trumpet that shall never call retreat; (*Speak, sir*)

He is sifting out the hearts of men before His judgment seat. (*That's right*)

O, be swift, my soul, to answer Him! Be jubilant my feet!
Our God is marching on. (*Yeah*)
Glory, hallelujah! (*Yes, sir*) Glory, hallelujah! (*All right*)
Glory, hallelujah! Glory, hallelujah!
His truth is marching on. [*Applause*]

References and Sources

Books

Anderson, Jervis. *Bayard Rustin: Troubles I've Seen, A Biography*. New York: Harper Collins, 1997.

Gaillard, Frye. *Cradle of Freedom: Alabama and the Movement that Changed America*. Tuscaloosa: University of Alabama Press, 2004.

Levine, Daniel. *Bayard Rustin and the Civil Rights Movement*. New Brunswick, NJ: Rutgers University Press, 2000.

Miller, Calvin Craig. *No Easy Answers: Bayard Rustin and the Civil Rights Movement*. Greensboro, NC: Morgan Reynolds Publishing, 2005.

Newspapers

Birmingham News, March 26, 1965.

Selma Times Journal, January 3, 1965; March 8, 1965; March 26, 1965.

Washington Post, January 31–February 4, 1965.

Web Sites

http://kamenypapers.org

http://web.archive.org/web/19990427180231/http://www.detroit-news.com/history/viola/viola.htm
http://www.lbjlib.utexas.edu/johnson/lbjforkids/selma-mont.shtm
http://www.mlkonline.net/ourgod.html
http://www.spidermartin.com
http://www25.uua.org/uuhs/duub/articles/violaliuzzo.html

Locations

Brown Chapel AME Church, 410 Martin Luther King St., Selma, AL 36703

Lowndes County Interpretive Center, operated by the National Park Service, 7001 US Highway 80 West, White Hall, Hayneville, AL 36040 (mile marker 106)

1.) What happened to Alan?

5961889R0

Made in the USA
Charleston, SC
27 August 2010